THIS SERIES IS DEDICATED
IN MEMORY OF MARTYN GODFREY.

Martyn, you wrote books that reached all of us kids at heart. You wrote them because you really cared. We all miss you.

MISSION 2

ALIEN PURSUIT

SIGMUND BROUWER

TYNDALE
KIDS

TYNDALE HOUSE PUBLISHERS, INC.
WHEATON, ILLINOIS

Visit the exciting Web site for kids at www.cool2read.com
and the Mars Diaries Web site at www.marsdiaries.com

You can contact Sigmund Brouwer through his Web site at
www.coolreading.com.

Designed by Justin Ahrens

Edited by Ramona Cramer Tucker

ISBN 0-8423-4305-9, mass paper

Printed in the United States of America

06   05   04   03   02   01
7   6   5   4   3   2

MISSION 2

ALIEN PURSUIT

CHAPTER 1

Ahead of me, somewhere in the jungle of tall, green bamboo-corn, a man's life depended on how quickly I could reach him.

This was no virtual-reality computer simulation program, like the ones I'd practiced for years in the science lab. It was the real thing. I'd been given so little time to get ready that all I knew were the basic facts about my mission.

The man's name was Timothy Neilson. He was a high-level medical tekkie—a technician who helped the scientists carry out their experiments. His job was to tend what we under the Mars Dome called the "cornfield," a large patch located in a greenhouse outside the dome. Neilson's emergency beeper had gone off fifteen minutes earlier, and it was a good thing I had already been in a practice rescue session, hooked up to the robot I was now controlling. That meant I could roll into action immediately. But I didn't know if that was fast enough. Timothy Neilson wasn't responding to radio communications, even though the computer link showed that his receiver and transmitter were both in perfect working order.

I knew one other thing about Timothy Neilson.

The emergency signal reaching the dome from a computer chip embedded in his space suit told us the suit was leaking oxygen and heat so badly that he now had less than ten minutes to live. If he was still alive.

The gigantic black shell of the dome was five minutes behind me across a stretch of hard-packed, red desert sand. That meant I'd have to find Timothy Neilson in five minutes and get him back to the dome in the remaining five minutes.

Two things would help me. First, I held a global positioning unit (g.p.u.) that allowed me to track the location of the signal chip in his space suit. Also, as I neared his body, I could switch to infrared vision and look for the heat escaping his space suit.

Even with the g.p.u. and infrared to help me, however, I was in trouble because of the bamboo-corn stretching high in all directions around me.

Although this was Mars, the stuff around me truly was as thick as any jungle. My mother is one of the scientists who has worked hard for fourteen years to genetically alter Earth plants that might survive on the surface of Mars. None can—so far—but these hybrids had come the closest. The stems of the plants were tall and thin and strong like bamboo plants, with wide, long leaves like those of corn plants. The entire field—a half-mile square of rows and rows of bamboo-corn—was enclosed by a huge greenhouse tent of clear, space-tech plastic sheeting that gave the plants the protection they needed to survive. With 100-mile-an-hour sandstorms that covered half the planet and an average temperature of minus twenty degrees Fahrenheit, life on Mars wasn't easy. But the next generation of these plants, my mom believed, would be able to grow without the greenhouse. In addition to the oxygen given off by the plants, the Mars Project would begin pumping oxygen into the atmosphere. Eventually, scientists hoped humans would be able to live on Mars without being under the protection of the dome. And that would help solve one of Earth's problems in the twenty-first century—overcrowding.

I was somewhere in the middle of this field, with four minutes now remaining to find Timothy Neilson.

Using my robot wheels, I rolled down a path between two rows of bamboo-corn. The leaves tickled like silk against my titanium shell. Above the rustling of those leaves, I heard the whistling of Martian wind as it found tiny gaps in the greenhouse tent. Unlike the dome, this wasn't sealed perfectly. It didn't need to be; the plan was to see if these plants could thrive with only some protection. If they lived, their seeds would be cross-bred and genetically changed again to make the next generation even hardier. I listened as the wind whistled and sand rattled against the plastic. . . .

No!

I told myself I did not hear what I thought I was hearing: movement in the corn leaves, just out of sight. Like the noise of dozens of creatures slipping away among the stalks of bamboo-corn.

I swiveled the robot body, scanning around me. But only the silent, tall green stems surrounded me like prison bars.

Then I saw a darting movement. But it came and went so quickly, I told myself it was just my imagination. *Aliens,* I told myself firmly, *do not exist.*

I pushed forward, wondering if those nonexistent creatures were about to attack me.

My g.p.u. chirped. Loudly. I would have jumped if I hadn't been on wheels. It chirped louder and louder, telling me I was getting close to Neilson.

Suddenly I came to broken plants, pushed over and sideways as if a man had crashed into them at a full run. I swerved and followed the crooked path.

It was easy to see footprints in the soil where the weight of the man's feet had crushed the wide leaves at the base of the stems. I rolled forward. It was like tracking an animal that had run in full panic, not caring what it hit as it fled.

As I followed a twisting path through the bamboo-corn, I had no choice but to believe something I did not want to believe. Someone—or something—had chased Timothy Neilson.

Impossible, I told myself again. This was Mars. The scientists claimed there was nothing alive on this planet that could hurt us. And aliens simply did not exist.

I quickly scanned in all directions, but the bamboo-corn made it impossible to see beyond the reach of my titanium arms.

I switched to infrared vision, which let me see heat instead of light. The green outlines of the stems and leaves against the pink light of the Mars sky disappeared. In infrared vision, I saw a blur of warm orange (the plants) standing on a deeper, brighter orange (the warmer sun-soaked soil), surrounded by a very light orange color (the cooler air).

Beyond the warm orange of the plants, I tried to sense the red shapes of living creatures.

Then I told myself I was dumb. Even if aliens did exist, which I knew was impossible, why should I expect them to have the same kind of body heat as humans?

The chirping of the g.p.u. guided me forward. I rushed as quickly as I could.

Seconds later, my infrared located the red outline of a space suit that was bleeding body heat.

Timothy Neilson.

"Are you all right?" I asked in my deep robot voice.

No answer.

I switched back to normal vision and focused on the white fabric of his space suit. He was lying on his stomach, his legs twisted beneath him where he had fallen in the middle of the bamboo-corn. His space helmet was hidden by the leaves of plants that had fallen on top of him.

I scooped him into my arms, grateful for the strength of titanium limbs. Without hesitation, I wheeled back toward the dome.

I now had six minutes and twenty-five seconds to get Timothy Neilson to medical help. *If* he was still alive. *If* I wasn't attacked by whatever had attacked him.

Because if I could trust my eyes, it looked like teeth and claws had ripped the holes in his space suit.

CHAPTER 2

"How is he?" I asked Rawling McTigre. Of anyone under the dome, he was my best friend. He was a mixture of father and buddy and teacher. I always felt I could ask him about anything, and I knew he'd treat my question with respect and honesty.

I was now disconnected from my robot body and back in my wheelchair, trapped by my useless legs. I sat in front of Rawling's desk in his new office. Until recently, the Mars Project director's office had belonged to someone else— the now ex-director Blaine Steven. He'd just lost his job because he'd nearly gotten 180 people killed (it's in my first diary). Now he was under guard in a small lab until the return ship could take him back to Earth. I'll bet Steven missed his nice office. Its walls displayed framed paintings of Earth scenes like sunsets and mountains. No bookshelves though. Cargo was too expensive. If people wanted books, they read them on CD-ROM.

"All Neilson's vital signs are fine," Rawling said in answer to my question. "The med teks tell me he's in a coma. He landed hard on his head and gave himself a concussion. If he comes out of it—"

Rawling stopped himself and sighed. "*When* he comes out of it, they expect he won't suffer any permanent brain damage from lack of oxygen. It looks like you got him back in time."

"Good," I said.

Rawling studied me with curiosity on his face. He had been a quarterback at his university back on Earth when he was younger, and his wide shoulders showed it. His short, dark hair was streaked with gray. He was one of two medical doctors under the dome, and he had recently been appointed replacement director of the Project. It might sound strange to say this, but even though he was in his mid-forties and I was only fourteen (in Earth years), Rawling was my best friend. Yet I was the only kid out of two hundred people here, so I didn't expect friends my age. Also, Rawling had worked with me for hours every day ever since I was eight years old, training me in a virtual-reality program that taught me how to control a robot body as if it were my own.

"All right, Tyce Sanders," he finally said after watching my face. "I want to hear *all* of it."

I should have known he'd figure out I'd kept something secret. Best friend or not, Rawling knew me almost better than anyone else, including my own father, whom I only saw every three years since he was an interplanetary space pilot.

"How did you guess?" I asked.

"It wasn't a guess," Rawling said dryly. "A man doesn't rip his own space suit to shreds. Maybe falling down a cliff with jagged rocks would have done it. But it couldn't have happened out there alone in the cornfield. There has to be more to it than what you told the med teks."

"I told the med teks the truth about what I saw," I said.

"But what I *didn't* say is that I wonder if he really was alone."

Rawling raised an eyebrow.

I described everything I could to him. The twisted, crooked path that Timothy Neilson had crashed through in the bamboo-corn. The big stretches between footsteps that showed he'd been running. And the sounds of creatures scampering among the leaves.

"That makes sense," Rawling said. "I don't want to believe it, but it makes sense."

Now it was my turn to raise an eyebrow. I was getting better at it. I'd sit in front of a mirror and work on raising one eyebrow, then the other. I practiced it because I liked the way it looked when Rawling did it.

"It makes sense?" I asked.

"I'll explain in a minute," Rawling said. "First, tell me why you decided not to tell the med teks."

"You're the director," I stated bluntly. "If there is something out there, I figured you should be the one to decide whether you want anyone else under the dome to know about it—in case people start to panic."

"From worrying about an alien attack?" Rawling queried.

"That would be big news for all of us," I responded. "Wondering what was out there and waiting. I mean, you saw what happened to Timothy Neilson's space suit."

"Just his space suit, right?" Rawling asked. "I know what the med teks told me, but I want to hear it straight from you."

All of a sudden I realized Rawling was talking as if there actually *were* aliens. Goosebumps chilled my neck.

"His body looked fine to me," I said. "So if they only hurt his space suit, maybe I showed up before they could finish the attack." I stopped and thought about what I'd said. "Whatever *they* are."

Rawling began to fiddle with a pencil on his desk. He spun it several times and spoke as he stared at it. "To find out there is other life in the universe beside life on Earth would be one of the most incredible discoveries in scientific history. Then to find out that this alien life-form will attack humans . . ."

He spun the pencil a few more times.

"Tyce, you know our last director kept too many secrets from people under the dome."

I nodded. Those secrets were another part of why ex-director Steven was heading for Earth on the next space-ship leaving Mars.

"Wrong as he was to decide who should live and who should die when the dome was running out of oxygen," Rawling continued, "he has some of my sympathy. Sitting behind this desk is not easy. Neither are some of the decisions." Rawling rubbed his face. "Conditions back on Earth are not the greatest. Because of overpopulation, governments are barely maintaining control as everyone fights for water and other resources."

"Yes," I said. I wondered why he was telling me something I already knew. Something everybody on Earth knew, too. Our presence on Mars was part of a long-term plan. Phase 1 had been to establish the dome. Phase 2, which we had just started, was to grow plant hybrids outside the dome so that more oxygen could be added to the atmosphere. The long-range plan—which could take over a hundred years—was to make the entire planet a place for humans to live outside the dome.

People on Earth desperately needed the room. Already the planet had too few resources for the many people on it.

If Mars could be made a new colony, then Earth could start shipping people here to live. If not, new wars might begin, and millions and millions of people would die from war or starvation or disease.

"What I'm saying," Rawling told me, his voice heavy, "is that if news of aliens—especially aliens that attack humans—reaches Earth, it might cause riots."

"I understand that," I said. I had never been to Earth myself, but I knew a lot about it from DVD-gigarom books. "Are you telling me there *are* aliens, and you've kept it a secret?"

"I'm telling you that if I do keep it a secret, people here might get hurt. If I keep it a secret, I'm doing exactly what the former director did. And I don't know if that's right."

He sighed again. "But on the other hand, if I call an assembly and tell everyone what I know, eventually word will get back to Earth and billions of people may panic. . . ."

I cleared my throat. "What exactly do you know?"

Rawling didn't answer. Instead, he flicked on his computer. The monitor on the edge of his desk lit up. I saw the cursor move across the screen.

"Here's why what you told me makes sense," Rawling said, opening a file.

It wasn't a text file or a video file, but an audio file. A short clip of excited shouting.

I didn't hear it right the first time. Or at least, I didn't want to believe I had heard it right.

"That voice belongs to Timothy Neilson," Rawling said. "It's his last radio communication back to the base. I've ordered the radio operator to keep it quiet until I can figure out what to do about it."

Rawling replayed the audio clip for me.

"Help!" a terrified voice shouted from the computer. It

11

was Timothy Neilson's voice. "Help! They're chasing me! Dozens of them! Help me! Help me! Help—"

All that followed those words of panic was static.

I stared at Rawling. Rawling stared at me.

"To make matters worse," Rawling said, "we're expecting the spaceship late tonight, with dozens of newcomers to the base."

CHAPTER 3

Some of you on Earth might already know about me. I'm the kid on Mars who was writing a diary about the final days under the dome, when it looked like everyone here would die. (See *Mission #1: Oxygen Level Zero* for that adventure.)

Even if you didn't read the long e-book of that diary sent by satellite back to Earth, you can probably guess that everything turned out fine in the end. Otherwise, I wouldn't still be writing, would I?

So why this new e-book, starting today, June 26, 2039 A.D.?

Mom figures anyone my age might be interested in a Mars diary, so as part of my ongoing homework, she's making me add to the first diary. If you feel sorry for me because you don't like to write, either, I'll thank you now. I wasn't happy with being forced to do it either.

Anyway, I'm not going to assume that you read my first diary and know all about me. So I need to tell you at least a little about myself; otherwise, you might be wondering how a kid in a wheelchair was able to see with infrared vision, move around in a robot body, and rescue a grown man like Timothy Neilson from certain death.

Let me start by telling you I'm the first person to be born on Mars. Everyone else here came from Earth nearly eight Martian years ago—fifteen Earth years to you—as part of the first expedition to set up a colony. During the eight-month trip, my mother, Kristy Wallace, a leading plant biologist, and father, Chase Sanders, a pilot, fell in love. Once on Mars, they got married, and I was born half a Mars year later—which now makes me fourteen Earth years old. Since the Mars Project director hadn't expected anybody to get married, much less have a baby, it made things on the colony so complicated that he decided there would be no more marriages and babies until the colony was better established.

There was no room on spaceships—which could reach Mars only every three years because of planetary orbits—for diapers, baby bottles, cribs, and carriages. And cargo was very, very expensive. So I had to do without most of that stuff. In fact, my wheelchair isn't even motorized, because every extra pound of cargo costs something like ten thousand dollars.

And the reason I'm in a wheelchair? Something went wrong in an operation on my spine when I was too young to remember. But you don't have to feel sorry for me. The operation and the wheelchair are the reason I'll be able to explore the universe in a way that no human in history has ever been able to do. You see . . .

"Tyce, are you cleaning up your room?"

It was Mom, calling me from the common living space in the middle of our tiny mini-dome. Like everyone else's, it had two office-bedrooms with a common living space in the middle. Mom wasn't able to use her second room as an office because that had become my bedroom. We didn't need a kitchen, because we never had anything to cook. Instead, a microwave oven hung on the far wall; it was used to heat nutrient tubes. Another door at the back of the living space led to a small bathroom. It wasn't much. From what I've read about Earth homes, our mini-dome had less space in it than two average bedrooms.

"No," I called back. "I'm at the computer. Doing homework. Remember? The homework you gave me?"

I guess if there's one good thing about writing my diaries, it's this: an excuse to avoid other things, like cleaning my room.

"All right, all right." I heard her laugh. "Can you wrap it up soon? I need to give you a haircut."

Like that was a good reason to hurry up and finish. I'd almost rather get poked by a needle than squirm under a sheet while she clips my hair and comes dangerously close to clipping my ears. And let's just say her haircuts are not a work of art. She's a scientist, not a stylist. Worse, because we can't waste water under the dome, we're only permitted showers twice a month. The rest of the time we use an evaporating deodorant soap. My next scheduled shower wasn't for another week. If she gave me a haircut tonight, I wouldn't be able to wash the itchy hair off my neck and shoulders until then.

"Haircut?" I hollered. "I just had one!"

"It was three months ago," she called back in an amused voice.

"No way! It's been only six weeks! I sure don't need one this soon."

Mom walked through the entrance into my room. With hands on her hips, she did her best to look stern.

"Don't lie. Three months. I marked it on the calendar because I knew you'd try to get out of it."

"I wasn't lying," I protested weakly. It figured as a scientist she'd keep track. "It was six weeks. Mars time." Here on Mars it took 687 days to circle the sun. Which meant a Mars year was about 1.9 times longer than on Earth. So my six weeks' Mars time and her three months' Earth time were about the same.

"Very funny," she said, unable to hide a smile.

"Wow," I said. "You look great."

"Don't change the subject." She smiled again.

"It's true," I said. "You do look great."

Mom had thick dark hair that was cut short, like an upside-down bowl. Normally, she didn't care much what she looked like—especially during the long, long months while my father was gone between refueling stops on Mars. It meant more to have a hairstyle that didn't take much fussing and gave her as much time as possible for her science. But tonight, her hair was done nicely. I could smell perfume, and she wore a dress I hadn't seen her wear since . . .

"I get it," I said. "Dad's coming home."

"Exactly. In about four hours. Which is why you're going to clean your room. And after that I'm giving you a haircut."

I pointed at my computer.

"Yes, yes. Finish what you were writing."

"Mom . . ."

In my mind, I heard Timothy Neilson's voice as Rawling replayed the audio.

Help! They're chasing me! Dozens of them! Help me! Help me! Help—

"Yes?" Mom asked when I didn't finish my words.

I really wanted to tell her about the aliens. Rawling had said I could if I wanted, because he trusted her, above all others under the dome, to keep the secret too. But she looked so happy about my father coming home that I didn't want to worry her.

"Nothing," I said, turning back toward my keyboard. But now I didn't feel like writing in my diary anymore. "Give me a few minutes to clean my room, and I'll be ready for my haircut." I forced a smile.

Clipped ears, in comparison to alien monsters that chased humans, suddenly didn't seem like such a bad thing.

CHAPTER 4

Four hours later, I was among those waiting outside the dome on the platform buggy—think of it as a clear dome perched on a deck that rides on huge rubber tires—to watch the landing. The Mars Project's other platform buggy sat beside us, empty except for the driver. The pilots, crew, and new project members would go back to the dome in that one.

I strained my eyes, looking upward. There was tension among us. While no previous landing had failed, there was always the potential for disaster. If anything went wrong, my father could die. Then the rest of us. Slowly. Because we were in the early stages of the Project, the spaceship was our only lifeline to the Earth. It had all the supplies we needed to survive another three years.

I reached down to the pouch hanging from the armrest of my wheelchair and pulled out three red juggling balls. Although it was dark, I began to juggle, keeping all three in the air without even thinking about what I was doing. Some people twiddle their thumbs. Me, I like to juggle. Rawling says I learned it because it's something athletic I can do better than most people who aren't crippled. He's probably right. I just know juggling makes me feel better if I'm nervous.

After five minutes, people began pointing upward. I let the juggling balls fall back into my lap and stared at the sky through the roof of the clear dome.

At first, it looked like a star growing brighter among the millions of stars in the Mars night sky.

It wasn't a star, though. NASA called it the "Habitat Lander."

The whole journey from Earth was complicated. My father and the rest had taken a Crew Transfer Vehicle from Earth, about a six-month trip through space. Waiting for them in orbit around Mars was the Habitat Lander. They hooked up with it and switched ships. Rawling McTigre had once explained it to me in Earth terms. It was as if they were crossing an ocean. They came over in a big ship, and once they reached harbor, a little tugboat took them the final distance to shore.

There was a difference, though. The journey had to be carefully planned so that it occurred when Earth and Mars were nearest each other—roughly fifty million miles apart. At any other time, their orbits placed the planets up to double or triple the distance apart. And little tugboats on Earth didn't have to deal with the intense heat of Martian atmosphere.

The bright light I now saw was the result of the Habitat Lander moving downward so quickly that, even in the sparse atmosphere of Mars, its bullet-shaped heat shield glowed with friction.

I held my breath as I continued to watch. There was silence around me in the platform buggy as everyone else did the same. We all knew this was not a simple tugboat operation.

Coming in at too steep an angle would fry everyone

onboard. Coming in at too shallow an angle would bounce them off the atmosphere toward Jupiter, without enough fuel to allow them to reverse and try again.

Although the Habitat Lander moved quickly, it seemed painfully slow to us down on the Martian surface. This was partly because it was still so far above us and partly because of our fear and worry.

Up there, my father was rolling the Habitat Lander to the right or left as it blazed through the upper atmosphere, steering it like an out-of-control sled careening down the steepest snow-covered mountain. Soon, too soon, he'd have to find a way to stop it.

I gasped.

The Habitat Lander's glowing heat shield, now appearing bigger than the sun, suddenly dropped straight down. My eyes followed as it flipped and tumbled, a blaze of fire heading directly toward distant mountain peaks. Then the blaze became shattered jewels of fire as it exploded on contact.

I took another deep breath, reminding myself of what I already knew but so easily forgot because this was only the second landing I'd witnessed.

That blaze was only the heat shield, discarded and dropped as part of the landing process.

I let out a breath of relief and searched the dark sky for what needed to happen next.

Retro-rockets.

Somewhere up there, if the Habitat Lander was still fine after dropping the heat shield, parachutes would have been released from the nose of the craft so it could land—feet first. Very soon, retro-rockets would kick in to help the braking process.

I found myself holding my breath again.

One . . . two . . . three . . .

Like a mushroom of flame, the retro-rockets burst into sight, maybe a mile above us. The burst drew our eyes like fireworks, and all of us on the platform buggy focused on it, following it downward.

I had my eyes open, but in my mind I was praying—talking with God. Some people might think he wasn't there to listen, but I had faith that he was. It was hard-earned faith, too. It came when I thought I'd die during the dome's oxygen crisis. When the crisis was over and I had a few minutes to reflect, I realized it's like this: When you get pushed to the edge of life and begin to wonder what's on the other side, your heart is really and finally open to believing that God is behind this universe; you begin to understand that he's as invisible and as strong as love. I prayed that God would be with my father and the crew and passengers in this final, dangerous part of the descent.

I kept praying as the flame of the retro-rockets grew to match the vividness of the sun.

And finally the outline of the Habitat Lander appeared above the brightness.

The retro-rockets pushed hard against gravity, and slowly the Habitat Lander settled on the surface of the planet. The parachutes sagged downward, covering the top of the space vehicle.

Cheers and whistles filled the platform buggy. They had made it safely.

I whispered a thank you to God. No Mars landing was easy.

But I was about to face something else.

Soon, I would see my father. For the first time in three years. Because his job was so important to him.

I couldn't help but wonder if he would be just another alien visitor.

CHAPTER 5

If you can picture an igloo, large enough to fit ten people, with that short rounded tunnel sticking out in front, you'll have a good idea of what the entrance to the dome looks like.

In our case, there are two large sealed doors to the short, rounded tunnel. The outer door leads to the surface of the planet. The inner door leads to the inside of the dome. Between those doors is a gap about twice the length of a platform buggy.

As we drove up to the dome, the outer door opened to allow both platform buggies inside the tunnel. When the buggies moved inside, the warm, moist, oxygen-filled air from the tunnel instantly turned into white, ghostly vapor and escaped into the cold Martian atmosphere. The inner door, of course, was still sealed to keep the dome's air from escaping.

As soon as both platform buggies, side by side, had entered the tunnel, the outer door shut behind us. Only when it was completely sealed against the Martian atmosphere would the inner door be opened. While we waited, people in our platform buggy waved at the newcomers in their platform buggy.

I tried to pick out my father among the people crowded in the other buggy, but I couldn't. Too many people were standing in front of me. And while a wheelchair is great because it always gives you a place to sit, the disadvantage is no different from being seated at a football game with everyone standing in front of you to watch a big play.

We had to wait patiently as a demagnetizing process cleared both platform buggies of Martian dust. We had to wait longer until the sealing process of the outer door was complete and both platform buggies had rolled into the dome. Then the inner door began to close and seal behind us, so that both doors now protected us from any air leaks to the Martian surface.

I was the first one off the platform buggy, lowered in my wheelchair with ropes by people on the platform.

Mom was waiting for me.

She stood beside me as other people poured out from both platform buggies and climbed down the ladders to the surface of the dome.

Finally, among the last people, my father appeared.

He climbed down slowly. After the weightlessness of space, even the weak gravity of Mars took some adjustments. It gave me time to look closely.

In one way, it was like watching an interesting stranger.

In another way, it was like looking at myself.

I was growing tall, just like he was. Mom would often point to his photo and comment that I was also beginning to look like him. I had dark blond hair like he did. My nose and jaws and forehead were bigger than I wanted them to be, and I hoped the rest of my face would catch up so that I would look more like him. My father was big, like a football player. I would be heavier and bigger too, if my legs didn't weigh next to nothing.

Mom stood by me, her hand on my shoulder, as we waited.

I knew she was happy to see him. I knew she wanted to run forward. But it was nice she didn't abandon me. *Unlike my father always does,* I couldn't help but think, *by always going off into space.*

He turned and scanned the crowd. I could tell the instant he saw my mother.

Slowly a big grin crossed his face, and he broke into an awkward half-run. He threw his arms around Mom and hugged her. Then he kissed her. She hugged him. Then she kissed him.

I turned my head. I mean, what kid wants to see his parents smooching?

Then something—or rather someone—caught my eye as I looked away from my parents' hugging and kissing.

The last person, back toward me, was climbing down the steps of the other platform buggy. Except it wasn't just a person. It looked like a kid about my age.

I could hardly believe it. I'd spent my entire life alone around adults; now there was finally someone my age!

The hugging and kissing continued beside me. My eyes however, were riveted on the new kid. What would he be like? Would we be friends? Was he hooked on astronomy like I was? Wouldn't it be cool to be able to share the stuff I was doing with a robot body?

I kept staring. The kid had short, black, straight hair. He was kind of skinny in the standard space uniform of a blue jumpsuit.

Finally, the kid reached the ground.

He turned toward me.

Except he wasn't a he.

He was a beautiful she. With dark eyes and high cheek-bones. Asian—and beautiful. (Had I said that already? The beautiful part?)

And when she smiled and her eyes met mine across the short distance between us, I gulped.

Wow.

CHAPTER 6

Was I ready to pursue aliens?

Yes, so ready that I got up early the next morning, though I usually hated mornings because I had a habit of staying up too late at night at the dome telescope.

After the arrival of the Habitat Lander, my parents had strolled around the dome together, arm in arm, talking for hours. I hadn't heard them come in because I was asleep, just like they were now, in the room on the opposite side of the mini-dome.

In my own room, I was up and restless because of what Director Rawling McTigre had decided yesterday. He intended to delay his announcement about the alien monsters for forty-eight hours. In that time, he hoped I might be able to find out more details, enough so no one would panic about the situation.

That meant that in about an hour, Rawling would send me back into the experimental bamboo-corn to search for the truth about the aliens. It was something I thought might be interesting to add to my diary.

I fired up my computer, rested the keyboard in my lap, and began to describe to my diary everything I knew about

Timothy Neilson and his run-in with the aliens. When I finished, I realized I'd forgotten to explain one simple thing—how, exactly, I intended to look for them.

So I went back to typing at my keyboard to finish my diary writing for the day.

Ever since I was eight, Rawling McTigre has trained me in a virtual-reality program. Any of you on Earth are probably familiar with it already. You put on a surround-sight helmet that gives you a three-dimensional view of a scene on a computer program. The helmet is wired so that when you turn your head, it directs the computer program to shift the scene as if you were there in real life. Sounds come in like real sounds. Because you're wearing a wired jacket and gloves, the arms and hands you see in your surround-sight picture move wherever you move your own arms and hands.

But here's what you might not have thought about when it comes to virtual reality: When you take off the surround-sight helmet and the jacket and gloves that are wired to a computer, you're actually still in a virtual-reality suit. Your body.

Rawling was the one who explained it best to me.

Your eyes deliver information to your brain. When you look through the telescope, your optic nerves take the image and fire it into your brain. Your brain translates the information. But your brain doesn't see. It relies on the extensions of the brain. Your eyes. Your telescope. Or the extension of virtual reality.

After all, your brain doesn't see anything. It

doesn't hear anything. It doesn't smell anything. It doesn't taste anything. It doesn't feel anything. Your brain is this incredible jumble of stuff packed into your skull that translates the information delivered to it by nerve endings. Some nerve endings are attached to the back of your eyes. Or to your ear canals. To sensors in your nose or on your tongue. To nerve endings in your skin and bones.

In other words, the body is like an amazing twenty-four-hour-a-day virtual-reality suit that can power itself by eating food and heal itself when parts get cut or broken. It moves on two legs, has two arms to pick things up, and is equipped to give information through all five senses. Except instead of taking you through virtual reality, a made-up world, your body takes you through the real world.

What if your brain could be wired directly into a robot? Then wouldn't you be able to see, hear, and do everything through the robot?

Well, believe it or not, that's me. The first human to be able to control a robot as if it were an extension of the brain.

You see, I'm crippled because of an experimental operation gone wrong that inserted a special rod into my spine. If you saw an X ray of my shoulders and neck, you would see that short, dark rod, hardly thicker than a needle, wedged directly into my spinal column at the bottom of my neck, just above the top of my shoulder blades. What looks like thousands of tiny hairs stick out of the end of the needle into the middle of my spinal column. Those are biological implants that have grown into my nerves. Each of the thousands of fibers has a

core that transmits tiny impulses of electricity,
allowing my brain to control a robot's computer.

This was part of the long-term Mars Project: to
use robots to explore Mars. Humans need oxygen
and water and heat to survive on the planet's
surface. Robots don't. But robots can't think like
humans. From all my years of training in a
computer simulation program, my mind knows all
the muscle moves it takes to handle the virtual-
reality controls. Handling the robot is no different,
except instead of actually moving my muscles, I
imagine I'm moving the muscles. My brain sends
the proper nerve impulses to the robot, and it
moves the way I made the robot move in the
virtual-reality computer program.

I admit, it's cool. Almost worth being in a wheelchair.

The robot is amazing. It has heat sensors that
detect infrared, so I can see in total darkness. The
video lenses' telescoping is so powerful that I can
recognize a person's face from five miles away.
But I can also zoom in close on something nearby
and look at it as if I were using a microscope.

I can amplify hearing and pick up sounds at
higher and lower levels than human hearing. The
titanium has fibers wired into it that let me feel
dust falling on it, if I want to concentrate on that
minute of a level. It also lets me speak easily, just
as if I were using a microphone.

It can't smell or taste, however. But one of the
fingers is wired to perform material testing. All I
need are a couple specks of the material, and this

finger will heat up, burn the material, and analyze the contents.

The robot's strong, too. The titanium hands can grip a steel bar and bend it.

Did I mention it's fast? Its wheels will move three times faster than any human can sprint.

"Tyce? Tyce?"

I'd been so used to hearing my mom's voice interrupting me that it took a second to figure out that the male voice coming from the other side of the mini-dome was my father's.

I saved my computer file and shut the machine down before I wheeled out into the common living area.

He was standing there in jeans and a T-shirt. He needed a shave. He held a nutri-tube in one hand, a mug of coffee in the other. "Did you get a chance to open the present I got you?" he asked.

"The CD with the top 100 rock songs of the 1900s?" I said. That was his music, not mine. Ancient stuff. "Looks great. Thanks."

"We can listen to it together," he said.

"Yeah. Thanks."

He sipped on his coffee. I tapped my fingers on the arm of my wheelchair. "Anyway," he said, "how are you?"

"Fine," I replied.

"Got time to share some breakfast?" He made a face. "Not that this artificial stuff comes close to a real breakfast."

"Wish I could," I said quickly, "but I've got to go."

"This early? Where?"

"Places. Maybe I'll tell you later, if I can."

He frowned. "What's the big secret?"

"Got to go," I said as I wheeled my way past him. I didn't care if he thought I was rude. After all, he'd been gone for three years. He'd be on Mars for only another few months until the orbit was in position for a return trip to Earth. And now he expected me to drop everything for him?

Not likely.

I had some aliens to catch.

CHAPTER 7

"Ready for those aliens?" Rawling asked, smiling.

"Which one would you like me to go after first?" I asked. "A slimy green one? Or a fat purple one?"

"Help out all Earthling kids," he said. "Get Barney."

"Huh? Barney?"

"You know, the fat purple one," he said, then stopped. "Sorry. Forgot you weren't brought up on Earth. You see, there was this television show where . . . and now I remember. It was a dinosaur . . . and it had been around forever . . . but it could have been an alien . . . and . . . ."

Catching my puzzled expression, he shook his head in disgust at himself. "Forget I even mentioned it. We've got serious business ahead of us."

We did.

As usual for all robot work, we were in the computer lab. I was on my back on a narrow medical bed. I wore a snug jumpsuit, in military navy blue. My head was propped up on a large pillow so that the plug at the bottom of my neck didn't press on the bed. This plug was wired to an antenna that was sewn into the jumpsuit. Across the room was a receiver that would transmit signals between the jumpsuit antenna and the computer drive of the robot. It worked just like the remote control of a television set, with two differences. Television remotes used infrared and were limited in distance. However, this receiver used X-ray waves and had a hundred-mile range.

"Let's go through the checklist," Rawling said. "I know, I know. We've been through this before," he said as I rolled my eyes. "But just like flying, safety is the first matter of importance."

With Rawling I knew better than to argue.

Rawling began pulling straps across my legs to hold me tightly to the bed so I wouldn't accidentally jump and break the connection between the antenna plug in my spine and the receiver across the room.

"First," Rawling said, "don't allow the robot to have contact with any electrical sources. Ever. Your spinal nerves are attached to the plug. Any electrical current going into or through the robot will scramble the X-ray waves so badly that the signals reaching your own brain may do serious damage."

Rawling tightened the straps across my stomach and chest.

"Second," Rawling said, "disengage instantly at the first warning of any damage to the robot's computer drive. Your brain circuits are working so closely with the computer circuits that any harm to the computer may spill over to harm your brain."

Rawling placed a blindfold over my eyes and strapped my head in position.

"Understood and understood," I said.

"Lastly," he said, "is the robot battery at full power?"

"Yes. And unplugged from the electrical source that charges it."

The robot was at the far end of the dome, near the entrance. Since the receiver worked at a distance, it wasn't necessary to keep it nearby. Before coming to the lab, I'd made sure the robot was ready for use.

"Good, good," Rawling said, squeezing my shoulder. "Any last questions before I soundproof you?"

"No," I said confidently.

"You're looking forward to this, aren't you?"

It was dark for me under the blindfold, but I grinned as if I could see Rawling's face.

"Big time," I said. The robot was a freedom that made up for my crippled body. No one else could wander the planet like I could.

"Then let's go." He placed a soundproof headset on my ears. The fewer distractions to reach my brain in my real body, the better.

It was dark and silent while I waited for a sensation that had become familiar and beautiful for me. The sensation of entering the robot computer.

My wait did not take long. Soon I began to fall off a high, invisible cliff into a deep, invisible hole.

I kept falling and falling and falling. . . .

CHAPTER 8

As I lay on the bed in the computer lab, light patterns from the other end of the dome entered one of the robot's four video lenses. Translated digitally into electrical impulses, that light followed the electronic circuitry into the robot's computer drive. From there, the electrical impulses were translated into X-ray waves that traveled through the dome to the receiver in the computer lab. From the receiver, the waves beamed to the wires in my jumpsuit, which were connected to the antenna plug in my spine. As the electrical impulses moved up the nerves of my spinal column into my brain, my brain did what it always did when light entered my real eyes and hit the optical nerves that reached into my brain—it translated the light patterns at the far end of the dome into images I could recognize.

A similar process also allowed the robot to hear—but through sound waves that reached my own ear canals.

No differently than thinking about moving one of my own arms, I thought about moving the robot arms. And instantly it happened. I brought both my titanium hands up in front of a video lens and flexed my fingers, wiggling them to make sure everything worked properly.

That's when the sound waves of a female voice entered the robot speakers and instantly entered my own brain.

Actually, it was more like the sound waves of a female scream.

I switched to my rear video lens. The image of a female jumping backward entered the computer and instantly entered my own brain.

It was her. The girl I had seen the night before was standing a few feet away from me. Evidently she'd recovered quickly from the scare of meeting the robot; she now stared with open curiosity.

As a robot, I was about her height. My video lens looked directly into her face. From this close distance, I saw her eyes were brown. She wore tiny, silver cross earrings.

I rolled my wheels forward a few inches and backward a few inches.

She jumped again.

"Greetings, Earthling," I said. The robot's voice box worked like a telephone. Although it was capable of sounding exactly like my own voice, words tended to come out more mechanically. In speaking to this girl in front of me, I dragged out my words and talked in a nasal tone, just like I'd heard fake robots talk in science fiction movies I'd watched on my DVD player. I don't know why I decided to do this; it must be just because I have a weird sense of humor and she was too new to the dome to know this robot was actually hooked up to a person.

"You can talk?" she said, surprised.

"Yes, Earthling. I can do many simple things. I can add two plus two. It equals four. Am I right?" I kept talking in that nasal, fake robot voice.

"Yes!" she said. "What about eight times eight?"

"Sixty-four, Earthling. Did you not know yourself such simple mathematics?"

"Of course," she said, folding her arms. "I was just testing you."

"Testing? What is testing?" I asked. This was fun.

"I guess if you had real brains you'd know, wouldn't you?" she replied smugly.

Ouch. I deserved that.

She stepped closer to me and looked me up and down. I knew what she was seeing.

The lower body of the robot was much like my wheelchair. Instead of a pair of legs, an axle connected two wheels. Just like a wheelchair, it turned by moving one wheel forward while the other wheel remained motionless or moved backward.

The robot's upper body was a short, thick hollow pole that stuck through the axle, with a heavy weight to counterbalance the arms and head. Within this weight was the battery that powered the robot, with wires running up inside the hollow pole.

At the upper end of the pole was a crosspiece to which arms were attached. The arms were able to swing freely without hitting the wheels. Like the rest of the robot, the arms and hands were made of titanium and jointed like human arms, with one difference. All the joints swiveled. The hands, elbows, and shoulder joints of the robot could rotate in a full circle, as well as move up and down. The hands, too, were like human hands, but with only three fingers and a thumb instead of four fingers and a thumb.

Four video lenses at the top of the pole served as eyes. One faced forward, one backward, and one to each side.

Three tiny speakers, attached to the underside of the video lenses that faced backward and sideways, played the role of ears, taking in sound. The fourth speaker, underneath the video lens that faced forward, produced sound. This was the speaker that allowed me to make my voice heard.

The computer drive of the robot was well protected within the hollow titanium pole that served as the robot's upper body. Since it was mounted on shock absorbers, the robot could fall ten feet without shaking the computer drive. This computer drive had a short antenna plug at the back of the pole, to give and take X-ray signals.

It was an ugly body, all right, but in her eyes probably better than the crippled body of a kid her age.

"What's your name?" she asked, smiling. She tilted her body left, and rested her right hand on her right hip.

I had to think quickly. I'd never thought of the robot having a name. I didn't want to give her mine. It might be fun to keep secret as long as possible that I was directing the robot from my real body.

"Bruce," I replied, grabbing the first name that came into my mind.

"Bruce?" She smiled again. I liked that smile. "How did you get a name like that?"

"From my mother," I said in a weird, slow robot voice.

From my mother? What kind of dumb answer was that? If I had robot legs, I'd have kicked myself.

She laughed. "Ask a dumb question, get a dumb answer. My name is Ashley." She stuck out her right hand. "It's nice to meet you."

I shook her hand with my titanium one, careful not to squeeze too hard. "Nice to meet you, too."

"Well," she asked, "could you give me a tour of the dome?"

A tour of the dome. I could get to know her as the robot,

and she wouldn't have to stare at my crippled body in my wheelchair. That didn't sound too bad.

"Later, please, Earthling," I answered. "When I return."

"Where are you going?" she asked, confusion on her face.

"To save all other Earthlings," I said. "It should not take me long."

I wheeled away and headed toward the dome entrance.

She waved good-bye, giggling—probably at how stupid I was.

CHAPTER 9

I wheeled outside the dome to a Martian sunrise.

I've been told that the sky on Earth is blue and the rising sun is yellow, with clouds around it colored pink, red, and orange. I've also been told that in the middle of the day, clouds are white, or if they hold rain, gray.

Not here on Mars.

The sun is blue against a butterscotch-colored sky. Later in the day the sky becomes red as sunlight scatters through dust particles at a different angle. At this hour, wispy blue clouds hung high in the butterscotch sky, but they'd disappear as the day became warmer.

Now, this early, it was cold—about minus one hundred degrees Fahrenheit. A sixty-mile-an-hour wind hit me, but it didn't have much force because the Martian atmosphere is so thin. Some blowing sand rattled against my titanium shell.

Once out of the dome, I felt free. I didn't have to wear a space suit. The cold and lack of oxygen didn't hurt my robot body. Best of all, my crippled legs no longer mattered. I was able to wheel across hard-packed sand toward the cornfield at the speed of a galloping horse.

Which I did.

Five minutes later, I stopped in front of one of the sides of the huge plastic-sheeted greenhouse.

Rawling and I had decided that the first thing I should do was check for holes in the sheeting. The greenhouse was designed to trap sunlight and heat. It was not designed to be sealed against the Martian atmosphere, so we expected that somewhere, along the miles of plastic sheeting, there might be a rip or two or twelve.

Slowly I made my way around the outside of the greenhouse. I wasn't just looking for rips, though.

I was looking for a place where aliens might have entered.

And fifteen minutes later, I found it.

More correctly speaking, I found tracks.

The hole itself was a couple of feet high and a couple of feet wide. It didn't have the smoothness of a rip. By zooming in with my video lens, I clearly saw scratches, as if a claw had been used to tear the clear plastic sheeting.

The sand below this hole was packed harder than the sand on either side. In the softer sand at the edges of this packed path, a few tracks were visible. The wind had begun to fill in the tracks with drifting sand, but I could still see enough to know the tracks were not my imagination.

They were about the size of the palm of my hand—my real hand, not my robot hand—and about half an inch deep. I could not make out any more details, however, because the sand had drifted.

I did know one thing for certain: The tracks were not human. And they led into the cornfield.

I spun back and followed the plastic walls of the greenhouse tent until I reached the same entrance I'd used when rescuing Timothy Neilson. The same entrance he'd taken when he went inside to check the growth levels of the plants, unaware that minutes later he'd be desperately calling for help.

It was much warmer in the greenhouse. Unlike the rest of the planet, there was enough oxygen in here from the plants to hold heat. That, combined with the greenhouse effect and the heat of the soil, made it above freezing.

Not that I cared one way or another. I was well protected by my robot body.

I rolled slowly inside, scanning in all directions.

As before, the tall bamboo-corn blocked my view. While these plants did need some water and the protection of the greenhouse, they practically thrived in the Martian air.

You see, while the atmosphere of your Earth is 21 percent oxygen, 78 percent nitrogen, and one percent argon and carbon dioxide, the atmosphere of Mars is 95 percent carbon dioxide, 3 percent nitrogen, and 2 percent argon and other gases. Humans breathe in oxygen and exhale carbon dioxide. Plants do the opposite, which is very handy. So plants give us what we need, and we give them what they need.

Since Mars is already rich in carbon dioxide, the plants only needed water to survive. And since Mars is such a dry planet, the plants were genetically designed to need very little of it. Any moisture they received was sprayed through nozzles from narrow plastic tubing that ran in grids along the ceiling of the greenhouse tent.

Because I could see so little, I followed the rows of bamboo-corn to the hole in the plastic sheeting.

It didn't help much.

On the outside, there was a packed path.

On the inside, the path disappeared, as if the alien creatures had scattered in different directions once they had entered.

That left me with too many questions.

Why had they entered?

Where did they go once inside?

Were they still inside?

Where did they go after they left, if indeed they had left the greenhouse?

Where had they come from?

And the most important question of all: Why had they attacked a human?

I wasn't worried about what would happen to me if they attacked my robot body. First of all, my titanium shell was a lot stronger than human skin and bones. Second, even if they were able to somehow damage my robot body, I could leave the robot almost instantly. In my mind, all I needed to do was shout *Stop!* The combination of throat and neck muscle movement from my brain impulses, plus the sound of that one single word, would trigger the computer drive to disengage me instantly, and my brain awareness would return to my body on the bed in the computer lab.

From the greenhouse wall, I decided to push into the bamboo-corn and try to follow one set of blurred tracks.

My hands and arms pushed aside stems of bamboo-corn. My wheels rolled over other stems.

I switched to my rear video lens and saw I was making a clear path through the plants. It was a straight path, unlike the one Timothy Neilson had made in his panicked run.

I realized something else.

My path was the only path.

Yet I was almost certain that some kind of creature had ripped a hole through the plastic sheeting of the greenhouse tent. I was almost certain that many of those creatures had entered the greenhouse tent. But where were the bent and trampled bamboo-corn plants that showed their paths?

The only answer I could come up with was that these creatures were small enough to move among the plant stems instead of plowing over them, like my robot body did.

But if they were that small, why had they frightened Timothy Neilson? Every person chosen for the Mars Project had passed dozens of tests; people didn't make it to Mars if they were wimps or cowards. Had the creatures frightened Timothy because he simply hadn't expected any other kind of life-form? And how and why had they managed to do so much damage to his space suit?

I followed farther into the bamboo-corn. I came to a spot where water from the nozzles at the ceiling had worn a small gully in the soil between the stems. Tracks littered the edge of this little depression. There was no water, of course. Even in the greenhouse, any water that didn't soak into the soil for the plants quickly evaporated.

A sound drew my attention away from the tracks at the edge of the gully.

A scurrying sound.

Then more scurrying.

I saw nothing because of the bamboo-corn that surrounded me, but the scurrying got louder.

I switched to infrared vision.

As with the last time I was in the greenhouse, I saw the different shades of orange that reflected the slight heat of the plants and soil.

Unlike the time I'd rescued Timothy, however, I saw shapes of deep red, the shapes of something alive.

Aliens!

Dozens of them!

Closing in on me from all directions!

I switched back to visual mode and saw only bamboo-corn.

Back to infrared.

I was about to be swarmed.

Any second these aliens would break through the screen of bamboo-corn that hid them from me.

I heard a click.

A hiss.

I strained to hear louder.

There seemed to be hundreds of the clicking sounds. The hissing became a roar in my sensitive hearing.

As the moving red shapes leaped upward around me in all directions, I switched to visual again.

I saw the darkness of moving objects in the air. Without thinking about it, I brought my titanium hands up to protect myself. I felt solid contact.

In the same instant, cold hit me.

And in the next instant, my brain seemed to explode.

It felt like I had run into a wall at full speed in total darkness.

Without warning, I began to fall . . . fall . . . fall. . . .

CHAPTER 10

I awoke to see Rawling McTigre staring down at me with concern on his face.

"Hello," I said with a croak.

"Glad you're back."

"Back?" I struggled to sit up. I realized I wasn't wearing my blindfold or the soundproofing headset. Nor was I strapped to the bed.

"Back?" I repeated. "Where did I go?"

"That's what I'm trying to figure out," Rawling said. "Your body didn't go anywhere, but you were out for six minutes and ten seconds."

"What?" I replied, startled.

"The computer shows the exact time that you disconnected from the robot body. Just over six minutes ago. Your body on the bed jerked around as if you had been shocked by electricity. You didn't make contact with any electrical sources, did you?"

Slowly, I remembered my last moments in the robot body.

Clicking. Hissing. Dark objects in the air. Sudden cold.

The sensation of hitting a wall at full speed in total darkness.

"Not that I know of," I said. "Not unless I was hit by aliens with electrical currents in their bodies."

As I told Rawling what I'd experienced, he listened gravely. Then he said, "It's a possibility. If they are alien life-forms, they might well contain strong electrical or magnetic forces. We just don't know."

Rawling helped me sit up. "The good news is, you have a clean bill of health. Your pupils aren't dilated. Blood pressure is fine. Heartbeat is normal. Brain waves are fine."

"We'll need the robot body to figure out what happened," I said.

"Sure. But it wouldn't be right to send anyone in there. Timothy Neilson was attacked by those things, and it took a robot to get him out. And now it looks like they were able to take down an indestructible robot body. If aliens managed to stop it, how much chance do we have to survive an attack?" Rawling took a deep, deep breath. "Here's the problem. We really need to know what those aliens are and what they're capable of doing. But I can't let anyone go out there if we don't know those things. And we won't know those things if nobody can go out there."

This was not good.

CHAPTER 11

After a very quiet and quick nutri-tube supper a few hours later, I decided to leave the mini-dome. My father and I weren't talking much. Mom seemed mad at both of us because we weren't getting along like she wanted. It was just easier to leave. It seemed weird in there, because my parents were so into each other. It wasn't that I was jealous or anything. Really. The guy goes away for three years, but when he comes back, he's the king. Me? I was suddenly useless and out of place. They had each other. All I had was a robot that I'd just named Bruce, and poor Bruce was stuck in the middle of a cornfield.

I decided to go where I usually went in my wheelchair when I wanted to be alone. To the telescope, far above the rest of the dome.

The good thing about living under the dome in a wheelchair is that I'd never had to travel far. The total area of the dome was about four of the football fields that I'd read about on Earth.

Besides the mini-domes (the small, dark, plastic huts where each scientist and tekkie lives in privacy from the others), there were experimental labs and open areas where equipment was maintained.

The main level of the dome held the mini-domes and labs. One level up, a walkway about ten feet wide circled the inside of the dome walls.

People mostly used the walkway for exercise, jogging in circles above the main floor below. Not me, of course. The tekkies had built a ramp for my wheelchair, and the only reason I ever went to the second level was to reach the third and smallest level of the dome, which anyone, including me in a wheelchair, could reach by a narrow catwalk from the second level.

This third level was centered at the top the dome. The floor of it was a circle only fifteen feet wide. It hung directly below the ceiling, above the exact middle of the main level. Here, on the deck of the third level, a powerful telescope was perched beneath a round bubble of clear, thick glass that stuck up from the black glass that made up the rest of the dome. From there, the massive telescope gave an incredible view of the solar system.

It took me less than five minutes to reach the telescope. I rolled into place where the dome astronomer usually sat and punched my password into the computer control pad.

When it prompted me to enter a location, I simply typed in the word *Saturn*.

With a whine of electric motors, the telescope automatically swung to find Saturn and focused on the planet.

I leaned into the eyepiece.

As always, I nearly gasped at the incredible sight of an intensely black sky filled with millions and millions of stars; they were so sharp and clear it seemed I could reach out and grab them. On Earth, the air and clouds and particles of pollution take away the sharpness of telescopes. But not on Mars, which has nearly no atmosphere. Looking through a telescope on Mars gives you the sensation that you are swimming through the universe.

Hanging in the infinite blackness was Saturn.

It wasn't the only planet I'd observed with rings—Jupiter, Uranus, and Neptune also have rings of sorts—but it was definitely the most magnificent.

To you on Earth, it might look like Saturn only has three rings. But from here on Mars, I saw differently. Saturn has thousands upon thousands of rings, gleaming in reflected sunlight. The rings aren't solid discs but are made of millions of pieces of "dirty ice," ranging in size from a grain of sand to an iceberg as big as a spaceship. Gravity holds them together, and they spin around the planet, some at speeds of fifty thousand miles per hour, creating a blur that looks solid to our eyes.

I don't know how long I sat there, marveling at those rings and the incredible sight. Long enough that I saw shadows of some of Saturn's moons drift across the face of the planet. Long enough that I began to pray.

You see, it wasn't until I faced death—I wrote about that in my last diary—that I allowed myself to have faith in God. I realized there must be more to being human than having a mind and body. I realized I have a soul, held within my body. Thinking of it that way has helped me deal with being crippled. You can probably run at a speed of eight miles an hour, but I can only roll along in my wheelchair at three miles an hour. In my robot body I can go three times faster than you can, but all of those speeds are so tiny compared to the vastness of the universe that it doesn't matter at all who's faster. What I've begun to understand is that I have a soul. And, in believing I have a soul, I was able to believe in

God. Of course, as Mom says, that's only the first step of a great journey. She says once you accept that, then each day is learning more about what that means. How God loves you, how you try to love God in return. And how knowing all of this helps you through the good and bad of life.

Looking through the telescope at the marvels of the universe, I now find it easier and easier to believe that God is behind it. That the creation of the universe was carefully planned out by God, and that he's still watching over it. Over us. It has given me comfort, too, to know that a lot of scientists look at the universe and say it points us to God.

Rawling is one of those scientists. He says a lot of things show that the universe was designed for the single reason of producing human life. It's something we've talked about a lot in the short time since he became director.

With Saturn there in front of me, so beautiful and awesome and stunning, it just seemed natural to close my eyes briefly and pray to God, thanking him for allowing me to see such beauty. It may sound strange if you don't pray much, but when I finished, I felt peaceful. I felt as if I did belong, I did have a purpose, and I was supposed to be part of God's creation. I felt as if a load had been taken off my shoulders; that since God made me and had a plan, maybe I didn't have to worry so much about things I couldn't control.

This peace lasted only as long as it took for one other person to step onto the third level near the telescope.

"Hello," she said. She did that tilting thing, hand on her hip, as if "hello" were also some kind of challenge. "I've been looking for you."

It was Ashley.

And this time I wouldn't be able to hide behind a robot body.

CHAPTER 12

"You've been looking for me?"

"Sure," she said. She grinned. It changed her. Without that grin, she looked grown-up. With it, she looked like a tomboy. "Everyone else here is ancient. Over thirty. I asked if there was anyone close to my age—I'm thirteen—and people told me about you."

She stuck her hand out, just like earlier when she'd introduced herself to the robot body. "My name's Ashley. Ashley Jordan."

"Tyce," I said, taking her hand and shaking it. "Tyce Sanders."

I was glad it was dim up here at the telescope. For some reason, my ears felt like they were burning red.

"Looked like you were sleeping at the telescope," she said, grinning. As if it wasn't a big deal that I was in a wheelchair. "Not that I was spying or anything, but when I walked up, you didn't hear me."

"I was . . . I was . . ." I only hesitated because, to me, praying was a private thing—and very new. But I decided I wasn't going to lie about it. There was no shame in trying to understand the mystery of life and seeing God behind it. So

I took a deep breath and explained. "I was praying. When I look through the telescope, it blows me away. I can't help but think and wonder about God."

"Cool," she said. She flipped back her hair, revealing her silver cross earrings. "I respect someone who's not afraid to ask questions about God and Jesus. There's so much to figure out," she said. "What I've found is that when you think about this universe as being *created* instead of just happening by accident, you start to see God everywhere, in all these amazing things. Wait until you get into Einstein's theory of relativity. Energy turning into matter. Matter turning into energy. Wow! What really messes with my mind is the relationship between time and the speed of light. Think about it. At the speed of light, time slows down to a stop. If you could ride a light beam across the universe, a billion, billion, billion, billion miles later, not one second of time would have passed for you, even though hundreds of years would have passed by on Earth. It makes me think that if God doesn't exist in the same sense we do in our bodies, it's only natural that he would be outside of space and time as we know it."

She laughed at my expression. "You can shut your jaw now. Your mouth is open so wide you could catch flies, if Mars *had* flies. What, you don't think a girl should know about stuff like that?"

I lifted my hand and pushed my jaw shut.

It made her laugh again.

"It's not that you're a girl," I said. "I mean, my mom's a scientist. It's just that I never expected the one person my age in this dome to turn out to be someone who loves science too."

"How could I not?" she answered. "Considering the family I was born into."

"What kind of family?"

She answered my question with a question. "What do you do for fun around here?"

If she didn't want to talk about her family, I wasn't going to push it.

"For fun?" I shrugged. "Dance lessons. Try out for Olympic sprinting competitions. Things like that."

"But you're in a . . ." She hit her forehead with the heel of her palm. "Sorry. You were joking, weren't you?"

Another shrug. "Bad habit," I said.

"Don't get me started on *my* bad habits. Let me tell you, six months crossing the solar system with no music or friends . . . well, halfway here I nearly asked for them to drop me off without a space suit."

"Um," I began, intensely curious but not wanting to pry, "exactly what *are* you doing here?"

"My father is a quantum physicist. That's why I know so much about relativity and stuff like that. He's setting up some research that's a lot easier here than on Earth because of the lower gravity. He's so good that when he told the United Nations' science agency he wouldn't go unless he could take me, they said it would be all right, since I was the only kid in our family."

Just like me. An only kid. And a science freak. Wow!

"What about your mother?"

Ashley stiffened, as rigid as a statue.

Dumb, I told myself. I'd just asked about her family again. "Sorry," I said.

"Don't worry about it," she said quietly, her eyes turned downward. "I'd have asked the same question. They got divorced about a year ago. It was just pretty messy, that's all. I think Dad wanted to be sent out here to get away from her."

"I'm sorry," I said—and meant it. I knew what having an absent parent was all about.

"Me too," she said sadly. Then she smiled, but it seemed forced. "You want to help me with something?" she asked.

"Probably," I said. With every passing minute, it was getting easier to be around her. I felt less shy.

"Help me find this robot," she said. "I met him earlier and . . ."

"Him?"

"His name was Bruce. He's kind of a smarty-pants, but it's cute."

"Oh, Bruce. You met him already?"

She nodded.

"Smart robot," I said, playing along. "Knows his math."

"I was impressed," she said.

"Wait until you catch his juggling act."

"Bruce the robot can juggle?" Her eyes widened like a little girl hearing about Santa Claus.

"Sure," I replied. "You'll know he really likes you if he offers to show you."

"Cool."

"Why do you want to find him?" I asked.

"He promised me a tour of the dome."

"He spends most of his nights plugged into the electrical grid," I said. I wasn't going to mention that this night he was lying in the middle of the greenhouse, destroyed by aliens.

"Oh. I know he's just a robot. But that sounds lonely."

"He'll be all right. He—"

I pictured the robot. Stuck in the middle of the bamboo-corn. At the edge of a small gully. A gully made by water from the nozzles of the greenhouse sprinklers. Which meant the robot was directly beneath . . .

"He what?" she asked.

I thought of the last things I'd heard and felt in the robot body.

Click. Hiss. Then something cold against the body.

"Got to go," I said and started wheeling quickly away from her toward the ramp. "Good-bye."

"But . . . ," she began to protest.

I didn't hear the rest of it. By then I was already whizzing down the ramp to find Rawling.

CHAPTER 13

I couldn't sleep after talking with Rawling about my theory. I kept thinking about what I'd be doing the next morning. So in the quiet of the night I worked on my diary.

I realized even if no one on Earth ever read it, I'd at least have it for myself. Years and years down the road, as an old man, I could reread all this and remember what it was like growing up on Mars.

Keeping that in mind, I pretended I was writing a letter to myself in the future. That made it fun as I finished explaining in my diary what had made me leave Ashley so quickly.

Aliens hadn't stalled the robot body.

It was water.

At least, that was my theory.

When Ashley asked me about Bruce—a dumb name, but it stuck—and when I thought about the robot beneath the water nozzles, the last sounds and sensations made sense.

Click. That was the automatic timer.

Hiss. That was the beginning of the water spray.

And the cold sensation? Water, of course.

My robot body had been standing at the gully where the water came down and collected. Water, then, had showered my titanium shell.

It was so obvious that after I rushed to find Rawling and tell him my theory, he groaned.

Rawling searched the computer records to find out exactly when I left the robot body and went into the thrashing fit on the bed. That time matched exactly when the automatic sprinklers in the greenhouse began to spray water. Which was not good for Bruce the robot body.

On Mars, it never rains. Water is a precious resource. The dome was established near the south, where we can get water from the polar ice cap. Because water is so scarce, no one bothered to wonder what would happen to the robot body if it got wet.

So what would happen to a robot body suddenly soaked in water?

An electrical short circuit. At least, if my theory is right.

In the morning, Rawling is going to try to hook me up to the robot body again. Then we'll find out more about the aliens.

It will only work, of course, if the robot body is still fine and we can get there before the automatic sprinklers turn on again.

But we won't find out until morning. And if it is fine . . .

"Tyce?"

It was my father's voice.

He knocked on the door.

"Yes," I called.

He pushed open the door. It was dim inside my room, with only the computer monitor giving light.

"Up late, aren't you?" He was framed in the doorway with light behind him, so I couldn't see the expression on his face.

"I'm not a kid," I said quickly. "Mom doesn't tell me when to go to bed anymore."

"Hang on," he said. "You don't need to get so defensive. I didn't say there was anything wrong with it. It was just a comment."

"In that case," I said, "you're right. I am up late."

"I don't appreciate your tone of voice."

Well, I thought, *I don't appreciate someone who shows up every three years and tells me what to do.* But I didn't say it.

I saved my file and clicked off my computer instead. When the monitor light dimmed, only the light from the common living area lit the room.

"Good night," I said. "I'm tired."

"Good night? But you were just—"

"I finished my computer work. I've got to get up early to-morrow," I stated flatly as I wheeled to my bed.

"Tyce, I don't understand why you act like this. I'm only trying to talk with you—"

I cut my father's words off. "Really," I said, "I'm very tired."

I heard him expel a breath. Then he left the room and shut the door without another word.

It left me in complete darkness.

For some stupid reason, I felt like crying.

CHAPTER 14

"Yesterday when you were out, I ran diagnostics through the remote and couldn't get a reading," Rawling said. His hair had rooster points, sticking up as if he hadn't had time to comb it yet. "But this morning everything checked out fine. If your theory about water is right, that would explain it."

We were back in the computer lab. I'd escaped the mini-dome without a lecture from Mom about how my father was doing his best and that he and I should try to get along.

I nodded in agreement with Rawling. "Whatever water leaked inside would have dried up after you ran the first diagnostics."

Rawling checked his watch. "The next automatic watering takes place in just under an hour. I want the robot out of the greenhouse before then. Even if you're not directly beneath a nozzle this time, you'll still get some of the spray."

Rawling lifted my legs onto the bed for me. He began to strap me down.

"Everything checks out fine with the robot. Still, I wish we could bring it in for a visual inspection. Any other circumstances but this . . ."

Again, I nodded. I felt sorry for Rawling. As new director,

this alien issue must be stressful. He was hours away from the deadline he'd set for himself to tell everybody under the dome about the aliens. If all he could tell them was what little we knew, it would raise the level of fear so high that his announcement could well do more harm than good. We definitely needed to find out more about those aliens.

"Rawling?"

"Yes?"

"I've got to ask. I've been trying to figure it out myself, and I can't get anywhere with it."

"Ask."

"You and Mom have been encouraging me to read some of the Bible." I paused, remembering how Ashley said she thought it was cool to search for the truth about God and Jesus. I echoed her. "It's been cool, learning about Jesus and thinking of him walking around on Earth and helping people and telling them about God."

"Yes?"

"Well, what if there are aliens? So far, we don't have any proof, except for what I might have seen, but that could be a water short circuit messing up the robot computer, or maybe me trying to imagine too hard I was seeing something. But what if there are aliens? Then how does God fit into this and all the stuff he promised through Jesus? Does God love aliens too?"

"Why don't you ask me the square root of 5,237,676?" Rawling fired back.

"Huh?"

He smiled. "Well, that wouldn't be much tougher of a question than your first one." He thought for a moment. "I'm not sure I can give you a good answer, Tyce. On one hand, it's God's universe and who are we to say what he can or cannot do in it? On the other hand, as humans, we naturally want to feel he loves only us in a special way. You have a special relationship with your mom, but does that mean that only she's allowed to love you?"

Ouch. So Rawling had noticed how I felt about my father. At least Rawling was being honest with me.

"Does that help?" he asked.

"No." I grinned.

He grinned too. "Never be afraid to ask questions about God. Even if it doesn't look like you'll get the answers right away. God is big enough to handle anything you might ask."

"Sure," I said. "Thanks."

"Ready for the blindfold?"

"Ready."

"Remember," he said as he put the blindfold over my head. "If anything feels or looks strange once you get in there, give the stop command and return here. Got it?"

"Got it," I said.

Rawling ran through our checklist.

When we'd reviewed everything to his satisfaction, he put the soundproof headset over my ears.

In the darkness and silence of waiting, I was nervous. If my theory was wrong . . .

I told myself that fear wasn't going to help me.

And as that thought ended, once again I began to fall off a high, invisible cliff into a deep, invisible hole.

I kept falling and falling and falling. . . .

CHAPTER 15

I stopped falling and opened my eyes among the stalks of bamboo-corn in the greenhouse. Light filtered into my front video lens. Mentally, I blinked. The robot, of course, had no need to blink the way I did in my human body, but it felt natural and brought the green of the bamboo-corn into focus.

I turned the video lens upward and brought the ceiling of the greenhouse into focus.

I'd been right.

Directly above me was a sprinkler nozzle. It would have completely flooded my robot body with water.

As Rawling had instructed me, I began a checklist of the other robot senses.

Sight, of course, was operational. I went to hearing next.

Without moving, I strained for any unusual sounds.

What reached me was the distant sigh of wind moving through small rips in the plastic fabric of the greenhouse tent. No scurrying of alien creatures.

And something else. Something strange.

I turned up my hearing volume.

There it was. A slow and steady and very soft *thump-thump-thump-thump*.

Like a heartbeat? Or heartbeats?

Sight and sound worked fine. Maybe too fine. The heartbeats made me feel like I was in some kind of horror movie.

"Hello?" I said.

My voice worked fine too.

My robot body couldn't smell or taste. So I let my mind go to the last of the senses. Touch.

I became aware of another sensation through my robot body.

Weight. And warmth. In my right hand.

The robot was so strong that I hadn't noticed the weight at first. To my senses, it was like a human wearing a watch on his wrist. Almost no weight at all.

But there was definitely weight, and definitely warmth, hitting the sensors imbedded in the titanium of my three fingers.

I slowly turned my front video lens downward. At the same time, I lifted my right hand upward.

At first all I saw was a blurry darkness. From looking upward at the ceiling, my focus had been set on a distance farther away. Like an automatic camera, the lens zoomed in to make an adjustment.

When I saw what I was holding, I finally realized where the sound came from, the *thump-thump-thump* that sounded like a heartbeat.

It *was* a heartbeat—from the small Martian creature gripped securely in my titanium fingers.

CHAPTER 16

I shouted *Stop!* in my mind.

Instantly I was back in my body. My human body. On the bed in the computer lab.

"Rawling," I said as calmly as I could.

I didn't hear his reply, of course, not with the sound-proof headset over my ears.

Seconds later, he took off my blindfold and removed the headset.

"You all right?" His face was worried. He quickly began to unstrap me from the bed.

"I'm all right," I answered. "And don't unstrap me. I want to go back. I just needed to ask you something. Not via robot. But person to person."

It felt strange, staring straight up at the ceiling while I talked.

"Ask away."

"Well," I said. This was going to be fun. Which is why I wanted to ask my question in person. "What do you want me to do with the alien I captured?"

"What!" Rawling shouted in my ear.

"Alien," I repeated. "I've got it in my hand. My robot hand. You want me to let it go? Or bring it into the dome?"

"Alien! What's it look like? How'd you capture it so quickly? Is it alive? Dead? Talk to me!" Rawling said excitedly.

I was right. This was fun.

"Remember I told you all these dark objects were jumping toward me as I blacked out in the greenhouse?"

He nodded.

"I'd brought my hands up to protect myself," I said. "One of them must have jumped into my hand. As the robot lost power, the fingers locked into place. The poor thing must have been stuck in the robot hand for nearly twenty-four hours."

"Poor thing?"

"Rawling, it's almost cute." I stopped myself. "Correction. It *is* cute."

I tried to think of a way to explain it. I had to rely on photos I'd seen in the CD-ROM encyclopedia.

"It looks like a mixture between a koala bear and a small puppy dog. It has thick dark hair, a mixture of brown and black. Not much for a nose. Big paws. Big eyes, two of them. Four legs. Two ears that hang down. A mouth, of course."

"But small enough to fit in your hand."

"Not really," I said. I had seen photos of people holding cats and dogs, so I had an idea of the size of those animals. "Bigger than a cat. I caught it under the front legs. Most of the body is hanging out of my hand."

"Alive?"

"Yes. But not really doing much. I think it's close to dead."

"Unbelievable," Rawling said. He drew a sharp breath, then let it out with a whistle.

"Believe it. That's why I'm back. I didn't know if you wanted me to bring it to the dome or not. I didn't want to do anything until I'd talked to you about it."

"Yes, bring it back," he said. A second later, he shook his head. "No. It might die in dome air if it's not used to breathing oxygen."

Rawling began to pace the room. "And what if it's carrying alien viruses or alien bacteria? If we bring it into the dome, who knows what damage those viruses could do to human bodies? Especially human bodies in a closed space like this."

He paced more. "But if it's close to dying, we need to try to save it. Do you have any idea what it would mean to science to be able to examine a living alien life-form?"

"How about if you drive a platform buggy out to the cornfield?" I asked. "Wear a space suit, and let all the oxygen out of the platform dome. I'll bring the alien out to you and you can examine it in the platform buggy."

Rawling stopped pacing. "Brilliant. Very brilliant," he said excitedly. "I'll take Jim Harrington with me. He's the best scientist we have in genetics."

With Rawling's praise, I felt proud—like he was my father. It was too bad my father and I couldn't talk like this.

"One other thing before you put me back in the robot body," I told Rawling.

"What's that?"

"When you leave the dome in the platform buggy, make sure you take some water for our little friend."

"Water?"

"Yes. Where I was standing was right below a sprinkler. I don't think those creatures were attacking me. I think they wanted water. When they heard the clicking of the automatic timer, they knew the sprinklers were about to start. I think they wanted to get at the water in that little gully before it evaporated."

CHAPTER 17

I opened my eyes again in the robot body. The little koala-bear alien was still in my right hand.

I rolled away from the gully and began wheeling toward the entrance of the greenhouse.

I stopped. Had I heard correctly? I turned up my hearing.

Yes. It was a mewing sound, coming from the little alien in my hand. I lifted it and looked directly into its large, brown eyes. With its last energy, it was trying to call out.

I heard another mewing sound answer from somewhere in the bamboo-corn nearby.

My visual only showed thick green leaves, so I switched to infrared.

There it was! A glowing red shape, maybe ten feet away, the size of the alien in my hand.

It was calling to the alien I was taking away.

I switched back to visual. The alien's large dark eyes made me feel sorry for it. I reminded myself that these crea-tures had attacked Timothy Neilson and ripped his space suit to shreds.

It mewed again.

"Sorry, little guy," I said in a soft voice. "I do not have

much choice. We will get you some water and maybe you will feel better."

Was it my imagination? It perked up at the sound of my voice.

I began to wheel toward the entrance again. The mewing behind me grew louder, and it followed me to the edge of the bamboo-corn.

At the entrance, I switched to the rear lens and looked for the other alien. It stayed hidden as I left the green-house, but the mewing grew louder, as if the creature was saying good-bye to the alien I'd captured.

Great, I said to myself. *Now I am a galactic bully.*

I turned my focus ahead, toward the dome. The sky had turned from early-morning butterscotch to a reddish-pink. The sun was a dark blue. The wind had dropped, and the temperature had risen. It was a great day to be outside on Mars in a robot body. A great day, that is, for sight-seeing.

But I had other duties.

In the empty space of Martian sand between the dome and the greenhouse, I saw the platform buggy on its giant wheels, racing toward me.

I headed forward to meet it.

As it got closer, I saw two men in space suits. I couldn't see their faces behind the dark visors, of course, but I guessed it was Rawling McTigre and Jim Harrington.

Dust sprayed me and the little alien as the monstrous vehicle lurched to a stop in front of me.

One of the space-suited men stepped out of the small, clear dome on top of the platform. He carried a Plexiglas cage in one hand and held the railing with the other as he climbed down the ladder.

When he dropped lightly on the ground, he opened the

cage without saying a single word of greeting. His visor was as dark as sunglasses, and I couldn't see his face.

"Rawling?" I queried.

Still silent, the man extended the cage toward me.

"Dr. Harrington?"

No reply.

The man in the space suit just pointed at the empty cage.

I obeyed his unspoken command and gently put the alien inside.

The man turned around and began climbing up the ladder.

"Is Rawling with you?" I shouted. "Can you tell me what is happening?"

The man ignored me and continued his ascent. Seconds later he entered the platform buggy's dome. And seconds after that, the platform buggy jerked forward, turned, and sped back toward the dome.

Strange. Very strange.

It looked like I was no longer part of this. Even if it did look as if I'd discovered the first alien life-form known to humankind.

CHAPTER 18

When I woke up on the bed in the computer lab, I was alone.

At least, I think I was alone.

Because I was blindfolded and wearing the soundproof headset, I had no way of knowing if anyone else was in the room. And because I was strapped to the bed, I couldn't move my hands to lift away the blindfold.

"Hello?" I called out into the dark silence. "Rawling? Anyone?"

I waited.

Nothing.

Five minutes later, still nothing. I was glad I didn't have to go to the bathroom.

Another five minutes, still nothing.

I shouted. "Rawling! Anyone!"

This was not fun. I had parked the robot body in a dry part of the greenhouse and given the stop command to return to my body on this bed. Now I felt like a prisoner.

"Rawling! Anyone!"

When the touch to my shoulder came, I nearly had a heart attack. The straps were undone first.

That should have been my first clue.

Rawling always took off the soundproof headset first, then the blindfold.

This person, however, began with the straps.

As soon as my arms were free, I lifted my hands and pulled off my blindfold myself. Then my headset.

"Oh," I said. "Hi."

"I was looking for you," my father said. "And from what your mom's told me about your recent virtual-reality simulations with the robot, I figured you might be at the lab. I'd just reached the door when I heard you call out. . . ."

"Thanks," I said.

"You all right?"

He looked tired and worried. I could tell he hadn't shaved yet, and his hair was messy. Because of all the love on his face, I wanted to tell him I was sorry for being such a jerk the night before.

But I just couldn't do it. So I simply said, "Yes. I'm all right."

"I thought you were always supposed to be under supervision," my father said, looking concerned. "Where's Rawling?"

"Right here." While my father and I were talking, Rawling had stepped into the room.

My father turned to face Rawling. "This is unusual. I thought he was supposed to be under supervision."

"Yes," Rawling snapped. "Believe me. This is unusual."

I struggled to sit up on the bed.

"What's happening?" I asked angrily. "Out there you don't say a word when you arrive with the platform buggy. I wake up here and I'm all alone. It's like once you had the—"

Rawling cut off my words. "Could Tyce and I speak in private?" Rawling asked my father.

"Not until you tell me what's going on," my father replied firmly.

"Look, I'm sorry," Rawling said. "I'll explain soon. But for security reasons, I need to speak with your son in private."

My father didn't reply to Rawling. Instead he said to me, "Are you all right with that, Tyce?"

I was glad he allowed me to speak for myself. I nodded.

"I'll go," my father told Rawling. "But I've already seen enough to make me wonder what's going on. Let me tell you this. Mess with Tyce, and you mess with me. Got it? As Tyce's dad, I won't fight his battles for him, but I'll fight his battles *with* him."

I was surprised at his tone. And suddenly, proud. I almost asked him to stay.

But he marched out too quickly, the anger showing in his quick steps and the straightness of his shoulders.

"You left me alone out there," I said to Rawling. "Then alone in here. And what about the alien?"

"There was no alien," Rawling said.

"Sure there was," I argued. "I saw you take it into the dome. It was—"

"There was no alien," Rawling said. "It's that simple. No alien. Now I suggest you go back to your mini-dome."

"But—"

"No alien. I refuse to talk about this subject with you anymore."

Despite his stern words, Rawling seemed to be quietly pleading with me. Confused by his sudden change in attitude, I wondered what was making him act this way. It had to be something beyond his control. Still, it made me mad. "Come on," I said. "You can't . . ."

"I can do anything I want. I'm director of the Mars Project, and I have almost unlimited authority. Please don't make me call security to escort you to your mini-dome."

With that, Rawling turned and left too.

CHAPTER 19

"Hello, Mr. Neilson," I said kindly to the man on the hospital bed. "Glad to see you're doing better."

If his condition hadn't been so serious—he'd been in a coma—I might have wanted to laugh at how he looked. He was completely bald, and his face sagged with wrinkles so that he resembled a round-headed basset hound. And his eyes were black and blue from where he had slammed against his space-suit visor.

"I'm glad to be doing better," he answered.

I nodded. "I have to tell you, when I picked you up in the greenhouse, it looked pretty bad."

I was probably fishing for a compliment, expecting he might thank me for saving his life, because he'd said so little since I wheeled into the hospital room to visit him.

"I don't know what you're talking about," Neilson replied.

Then I realized he'd hit his head hard enough to knock himself out. The space suit had lost air and heat. No wonder he couldn't remember. So I tried to fill him in.

"No one told you? You were in the greenhouse. Something was chasing you. You fell down. Your space suit was ripped. They sent a robot in to get you."

"It's not good to make up stories," Neilson said, frowning at me.

"I'm not," I insisted.

"I was collecting rock samples," he explained. "I fell and tumbled for quite a distance. Jagged rocks ripped my space suit. Meds in a platform buggy rescued me."

Why was he lying? Nobody collected rock samples in the greenhouse.

"I was there," I said. "I saw different."

"You were there? A kid in a wheelchair?"

"I mean I was there, controlling a robot body. I saw the path in the greenhouse where you'd been running."

"Not true."

"But I can prove it. There was a voice recording. You said something was chasing you. I heard it. That's why I'm here. To ask you about that."

"You're mistaken. Stop bothering me with this nonsense. I need to rest."

"Nonsense? It's not nonsense. It's—"

"Med! Med!" Timothy Neilson called loudly to another room. "Could you ask this young man to leave? He persists in bothering me."

Seconds later, a large man appeared with Rawling behind him.

"Tyce," Rawling said sternly, "this man needs recovery time. He took a bad spill down a cliff. Maybe you should go now."

"Down a cliff! Come on. He was in—"

"Enough, Tyce," Rawling warned me. "Say good-bye."

I could tell it was useless to argue.

"Furthermore," Rawling continued, "I suggest you talk about this with no one else. Including your parents."

"Or else?" I said angrily, not believing this was the Rawling I'd known for years. What had gotten into him?

"Or else they will be shipped back to Earth," he said bluntly.

I turned my wheelchair and pushed past him.

I was getting kicked out. Just like a half hour earlier, I'd been kicked out of Dr. Harrington's office when I'd gone to ask him how the alien was doing.

Now I was really, really mad.

CHAPTER 20

I was beginning to find that writing in my diary helped me get my thoughts straight. Early in the evening, instead of going to the telescope as I often did, I stayed in our mini-dome and began to type on the keyboard.

I wrote all the things I knew for sure about what had happened.

> Earlier in the day I captured an alien. Two men in space suits met me in a platform buggy and took the alien into the dome. Since then Rawling has pretended the alien doesn't exist. Dr. Harrington refuses to talk to me. Timothy Neilson acts like he wasn't attacked by these aliens.

I was in the middle of a big stretch and yawn when I thought of something else. I banged away at my keyboard.

> Something is strange. Rawling told me he didn't want the alien inside the dome because our air might kill it and because it might have alien viruses or alien bacteria that might hurt humans. But the

men in the space suits immediately took the alien
into the dome. Does that mean they already knew
it was safe for the alien and for us? And if it is
safe, could that mean it isn't truly an alien?

That's as far as I got with my diary. I knew who could
help me with this question.

"Mom!" I shouted. "Mom!"

I pushed away from the computer and rolled toward my
door.

"Mom! Mom!"

She met me at the doorway.

"I have to ask you something!"

"That's it? Yelling like that and all you have is a question?"

"A big question. About genetic experiments."

Mom moved to my bed and sat on the edge. I wheeled
around to face her.

"How does it work? When you try to make a different
kind of plant? You know, the DNA and stuff like that."

"How long an answer do you want?"

"Short. Like an overview."

She nodded. "Picture a circle with a dot in the center."

"Done."

"That's a simple drawing of a cell under a microscope.
The circle is the outer wall. Everything inside the circle and
around the dot is a plasma with nutrients. The dot in the
center is the nucleus. The nucleus is the computer software that runs the cell. Got it?"

"Got it."

"As a biologist, I can only marvel at how God has made
the nucleus so simple, yet so complex. It contains the DNA
you mentioned, which is microscopic strands of protein.

This protein is in the form of a double helix, which is the shape of a ladder that has been twisted into a spiral. Still with me?"

"Still with you."

"The double helix shape lets the DNA duplicate perfectly, so that one cell can photocopy itself a trillion times and it will still be a perfect copy, no mistakes. That's important to genetic experiments. Very important."

"Important," I said.

"Let's talk about flies, for example. Every creature, including a human, begins as one cell. That cell divides and divides and divides. As it divides, the DNA of the cells programs the different cells to specialize. Some cells become skin cells, other cells become eye cells, and so on."

"I'm listening."

"What's absolutely mind-bogglingly amazing," she said, showing her excitement for her work, "is that the DNA packed into that single first cell contains the entire genetic code for that creature or plant. One cell, hundreds of times smaller than the head of a pin, contains the blueprint to build a fly. Or a sheep. Or a monkey. DNA is incredible. That's partly why I first began to believe in God—because it was too difficult to believe that something this amazing could develop by accident."

I nodded. "Experiments . . ."

"Yes. Experiments. Decades ago, back in the twentieth century, scientists realized it would be very simple to change a species. All they had to do was change the DNA when it was at the one-cell stage. Let me put it this way. Is it easier to change a trillion cells, or is it easier to change the original cell and let the changes in that first cell be programmed into every cell as it divides?"

"No-brainer," I said. "Get to the first cell."

"That's what they did. I remember reading about one of the first genetic experiments on fruit flies. Scientists changed the DNA that programmed eye growth. When these flies hatched, they had up to fourteen pairs of eyes. Eyes on their legs, wings, backs, chest. Scientists had created mutant flies."

"Wow."

"Then in the 1990s scientists learned how to clone animals, and suddenly genetics became scary. It was possible to literally create new species."

"Could they do this to humans?"

Mom rubbed her face. "Yes. Even before the year 2000, the technology to do this was possible. And then the worst happened. An unethical scientist not only cloned humans but also experimented on them to make them taller and stronger. They nicknamed him 'the new Dr. Frankenstein.' He made a mistake, however, and his clones were born without arms. That was in 2010 A.D. It made such an uproar that the government finally stepped in. Very strict laws were created and enforced."

"But," I said, "it is *possible* to try to create new species."

"It's possible. For the last thirty years, however, continuing public outrage has made it difficult for scientists on Earth to get funding for any genetic experiments of that type." She smiled. "Plant experiments are one thing, but on animals, no way. Just like smoking in public places or drinking and driving, it has become unthinkable."

"On Earth," I said thoughtfully. "Unthinkable on Earth."

She snorted. "Unthinkable anywhere in the solar system. If anyone tried it on Mars and the public on Earth found out, it would threaten the billions and billions of dollars of government support needed to keep this project going forward."

"Thanks," I told her.

"Why are you asking all of this?"

"Curiosity," I answered. "And you've been a big help."

She had been. Genetic experiments to create an animal that would survive on Mars would be top secret.

Now I had to find a way to prove that those experiments existed.

CHAPTER 21

"Greetings, Earthling."

I had found Ashley in the same spot I always went when I wanted to be alone. Up at the telescope.

She jumped. "Bruce!"

"Yes, Earthling. You remember me, then."

I was in the robot body, of course. Back in the computer lab, in my wired jumpsuit, I had set up the software by myself. My own body was in the wheelchair, with the blindfold and headset I'd put on myself. The only risk I was taking was that I might move in the wheelchair and break the connection. If that happened, I convinced myself it would not damage my body. I hoped. And I also hoped that Rawling wouldn't stop by the lab during the time I was hooked up to the robot's body.

"Remember you? Certainly. You promised me a tour of the dome."

"You will have your tour, Earthling," I continued in my cheesy robot voice. "However, I wish for you to help me first."

"Sure. It's not like I have anything else to do." Ashley

put her hand on my robot shoulder. "That kid Tyce was talking about you. Do you know him?"

"Yes, Earthling. A very fine human specimen. Smart. Handsome. Witty. You would do well to spend much time with him."

"Huh. Last time we talked, he ran away."

"It must have been important business," I said. "Perhaps later tonight you will see him."

"Well," she said, smiling, "there is a reason I was waiting up here. Not many guys I know can talk science like he does."

"Perhaps you find him to be, as you humans say, appealing in a handsome way?"

"What kind of robot are you?"

I decided to change the subject. "One in need of help. Please."

"Back to that again. What would you like me to do?"

I explained in my finest nasal robot voice.

She agreed.

CHAPTER 22

Five minutes later, I was on the Martian landscape.

I had needed Ashley to help me leave the dome. Alongside the large doors that allowed platform buggies to come in and out, there was a set of small doors to give entrance or exit for men and women in space suits. Ashley had punched in the number sequence on the control pad and promised to wait to let me in when I returned.

I did not expect it to take long. I needed five minutes to get to the greenhouse, five minutes to return, and however long it would take me inside to accomplish my mission.

My wheels whirred along the hard-packed sand. The Martian sky was dark. A ghostly white object whizzed overhead. Phobos—one of the Martian moons. I knew if I waited outside, soon I would see Deimos, the other moon, whizzing in the opposite direction.

But I wasn't going to wait.

I had a small cage in one hand and a container of water in the other.

I was gambling that I knew why the alien creatures stayed in the greenhouse. I believed they needed the oxygen given off by the plants to survive, as well as the water that came down from the automatic sprinklers.

If I was right about a few things, it wouldn't take me long to capture another one.

And I was right, at least about one thing.

There were more of them inside. Or at least one.

Within a minute of going inside, among the darkness of the plants, my infrared spotted a tiny red glow. It was exactly where I'd left behind the second alien earlier. As if it was waiting for its friend to return.

Would I be right about my second guess?

Since the robot body gave off no heat and no human smell, I hoped the creatures wouldn't be afraid of it.

As for my third guess, I'd find out as soon as I opened the water container.

I set the cage down, opened the water container, and set it inside the cage.

I did not back away from the cage. If my second and third guesses were right . . .

My infrared showed the second alien moving closer, at first slowly, then quickly. Had it smelled the water?

Yes!

It came out of the darkness of the bamboo-corn and into the open.

Would it be afraid of the presence of my robot body?

No!

It moved almost to the cage, so close that I could have bent down and grabbed it.

I didn't, of course. I wanted it in the cage.

Ten seconds later, it stepped inside and began to lap at the water.

I saw the red glows of other creatures approaching,

drawn by the water they must have sensed as it evaporated quickly in the dry atmosphere.

All I needed, however, was one. This one. The friend to the one I had captured earlier.

I snapped the cage shut before the creature could back away from the water.

I had it!

The first step of my plan had gone off without a hitch.

Unfortunately, that was only the beginning of what I needed to do during the rest of the evening.

CHAPTER 23

"Perhaps, Earthling, we shall tour the dome later."

I was back inside, with my robot body carrying the cage. But Ashley wasn't listening to Bruce. Her attention was on the cage.

"What is that?" she asked, pointing.

"A lost, lonely Martian animal," I said.

"An alien!"

"A lost, lonely Martian animal. Are you deaf?"

Ashley shook her head in evident disgust at the robot and the robot voice. "Whoever it was who made you smart enough to talk to people should have done something about that voice."

"Earthling is not funny," I said.

She was ignoring me again, trying to look in the cage. Fortunately, it was midevening, and most of the scientists and tekkies were in their mini-domes. I had counted on that.

"Please take this to the kid named Tyce," I said. "You will find him at the ramp that leads up to the second level."

I handed her the cage.

"Earthling, do not open it," I said.

"And I'm tired of this 'Earthling' stuff. My name is Ashley."

It was my turn to ignore her. I spun around and wheeled away.

"Hey!" she said. "Come back here!"

Too late. I was gone.

⚛

I blinked open my eyes in the wheelchair in the computer lab.

I had parked Bruce the robot at his power charger. Later tonight, I'd plug him in. But now I had to make it to the bottom of the ramp as quickly as possible.

I gripped the wheels of my chair and shoved forward. My legs might be useless, but any of the scientists or tekkies who arm-wrestled me always lost. I worked my arms hard as I raced to meet Ashley at the bottom of the ramp.

I could see her ahead in the dimness of the lights set at evening level. She stood near the ramp, looking in all directions. The cage was at her feet.

Seconds later, I pulled up.

"Hello," I said.

"Oh hello, Mr. Rude," she said sarcastically, her hands on her hips. "Going to take off on me again without any warning? Between you and that dumb robot, it's enough to—" She stopped as she noticed what I was doing.

"Hey! Bruce told me not to open the cage. You can't—"

I'd already done it—opened the cage.

The little Martian creature crawled forward. It paused for a second, then scampered away.

"I can't believe you just did that," Ashley said. "Now what are we going to do?"

"Follow," I said calmly. "Think you can keep up with me?"

"Sure, but how are you going to follow it?"

I grinned and pulled a handheld computer unit from my lap.

"It's called a g.p.u."

"Geepeeyew?" she parroted back.

"Global positioning unit. Works off satellites that circle Mars."

"Great. What are you going to do? Throw it at that thing? It's long gone."

I flicked on the switch. Immediately, it began beeping.

"Come on," I told Ashley. "This should be fun."

CHAPTER 24

It *was* fun.

While I was in the robot body, crossing the Martian sand from the greenhouse tent back to the dome, I had attached an emergency tracking device onto the back of the furry, little Martian koala. It meant that now I'd be able to track it wherever it went in the dome.

I hoped that if it was able to smell water, it would also be able to smell its partner, the little guy I'd taken away from it.

Beep-beep-beep-beep.

I left the g.p.u. in my lap as I wheeled forward. Ashley stayed close behind. The signal grew louder as we neared the laboratories at the far end of the dome.

"What's this about, anyway?" Ashley asked.

"I'm not 100 percent sure," I said. "But I think it's about illegal experiments and some people trying to hide those experiments."

I kept pushing as I spoke. I thought about the rod in my spine—and how the operation that had placed it there had left me crippled. "Someday I'll tell you what it's like to be experimented on when you aren't given the chance to decide for yourself." Just as I suspected that someone was experimenting on the Martian koalas.

Beep-beep-beep-beep. The signal grew louder and quicker.

We were almost there. We faced a row of laboratory doors.

Beep-beep-beep-beep.

"Look!" Ashley exclaimed.

I looked where Ashley was pointing.

At the far end of the row, the little Martian creature scratched at a door.

I pulled up.

The sign on the door had big bold letters: **Authorized Personnel Only.**

"Try the door handle," I suggested.

"I'm not authorized."

"Neither is the little guy trying to get in."

"He's got an excuse. He can't read," she fired back.

I liked her. She was quick. "Fine, then," I said. "Neither can I."

She sighed and tried the handle. It was locked.

I leaned forward and knocked on the door.

"Go away," a voice shouted from inside.

I knocked louder. This time, no voice answered.

"Inside that room," I told Ashley, "are things that aren't supposed to be happening. For all we know, the person inside is trying to kill and/or hide all the experimental animals."

"Who can we report this to?" Ashley said, shocked.

"No one," I answered. I felt bitter and sad about Rawling McTigre. By now I'd figured that he was involved somehow. "The director of the Mars Project isn't even interested in stopping this."

"Who else knows about it?"

"You and me."

"Do you think," she asked, "if more people knew what was inside, we could stop this?"

"Maybe," I answered. "Should we try to break down the door?"

The little creature at our feet clawed and scratched to get in.

"No." She grinned. "I've got a better idea."

She tilted her head back and screamed, louder than I knew any person could scream. She screamed as if a madman were chasing her down. She screamed as if she were in a spaceship headed directly for an asteroid. She screamed as if a huge alien had pulled off one of her arms.

I plugged my ears.

She kept screaming.

It worked.

All across the dome, lights began to flick on.

Within thirty seconds, dozens of people were running toward us.

She finally stopped. And grinned. "Not bad, huh?"

I grinned back. "Not bad at all."

CHAPTER 25

By the time I was ready for sleep, I wasn't ready for sleep.

Sure, the clock said it was late, but I was still too excited from all the things that had happened since Ashley screamed to the world.

I'd already explained everything to my parents. Now they were asleep, and the mini-dome was quiet.

That left me one thing I could do—write in my diary and explain it to the old man I would someday become. I fired up my computer and began to tell the rest of it.

Ashley's scream brought dozens of people. Many of them wore pajamas because they'd been asleep or were getting ready to sleep. The little Martian koala was still trying to get inside the door, and that was all the proof we needed to convince everyone that inside the lab we'd find at least one more.

It turned out there were dozens in plastic boxes that had been their homes. By the time we got the door open, most of them had been crammed into a storage box.

Dr. Jim Harrington, the head scientist on the illegal experiment, had figured he'd been caught and was trying to get rid of the evidence. We'd stopped him just before he was about to load the genetically altered koalas on a platform buggy and drive them miles and miles away from the dome. He'd planned to leave them to die, trapped in the box. Now it's going to be up to the director to decide what to do.

I finished my keyboarding.

What *would* the director do?

In the morning, I was going to find out. Because I intended to sit in Rawling's office until he told me everything else.

I shut off my computer and wheeled over to my bed. I pulled myself out of my wheelchair and got under the covers, then reached over to shut off the light.

I laid awake in the darkness, thinking about everything.

But I wasn't alone.

Happy mewing sounds came from a basket in the corner of the bedroom. The two little Martian koalas the robot had captured were snuggled against each other.

I wasn't quite sure what to name them yet. I was just happy that they were finally back together.

Five minutes later, they began to snore.

Wonderful.

CHAPTER 26

I found Rawling McTigre at his desk. He lifted his head as I rolled in.

"Good morning," he said.

"If you say so."

He nodded. "You have every right to be mad at me."

"Why should I be mad? Just because you suddenly pretend I don't exist? And that the alien I found doesn't exist? I thought that's what friends always did to each other."

Rawling sighed and stood. He took a piece of paper from his desk and walked it over to me.

"My letter of resignation as director," he said, handing the paper to me. "Take a look at the date."

I scanned the letter. It was very short and very polite. It was dated yesterday.

"So?" I asked.

"I wrote it and signed it yesterday afternoon. Before you found the experimental lab. Not after. You probably don't trust me anymore—and I don't blame you—so I can bring up the computer file and show you the last time I worked on the letter to prove I'm not lying."

I gave him back the letter.

"Tyce," he said, his voice softening, "it's important to me that you know I resigned because of what was happening. I was on my way over to explain to you last night when all that screaming brought us to the lab."

Rawling returned to his desk, sat down, and faced me. "Here it is in a nutshell. Yes, unethical secret experiments had been performed with the blessing of the previous director, Blaine Steven. Dr. Harrington's goal was to take an Earth species and genetically alter it to survive on Mars. He picked koalas because they survive on vegetation and have a relatively low consumption of energy. His ultimate goal was to create a creature that needs low oxygen, builds a thick layer of fat and fur to protect it against cold, and will eat the bamboo-corn that will be planted around the planet."

"Why?" I asked.

"Dr. Harrington claims the koalas are intended to be a future food source. But I'm not sure I believe him."

"Because . . . ," I said slowly as I processed this information.

"I'll get to that in a minute. It's one of the reasons I resigned. But I want to explain what they were doing out in the cornfield."

I nodded. Rawling looked weary. I didn't know whether to feel sorry for him or stay angry.

"Remember the oxygen crisis in the dome? Remember how ex-Director Steven arranged for oxygen tanks to be stolen?"

I nodded again.

"You might not have noticed," Rawling said, "but twenty tanks were stolen, and later only eighteen were recovered. I finally found out where the missing two tanks went. To the secret experimental lab. Steven had approved it to keep as many of the experimental animals alive as possible."

"Instead of trying to keep scientists or tekkies alive?"

"Steven and Harrington thought people were going to die anyway. So why not at least keep alive these important experiments?"

I shook my head in disgust.

"At that time," Rawling continued, "Dr. Harrington realized he didn't have enough oxygen for all his animals to survive. So he released most of them onto the surface of the planet, expecting them to die. He didn't realize how close this new generation was to being able to survive outside of the dome. The creatures survived long enough to make it to the greenhouse tent, which evidently had just enough traces of oxygen and water to keep them alive."

I was beginning to understand. "Which Harrington did not know until Timothy Neilson was attacked in the cornfield—"

"Not exactly attacked," Rawling said. "These animals are vegetarians. But they were desperate for water. You know no space suit is completely sealed down to a microscopic level. These creatures could smell the trace amounts of moisture that leaked from Neilson's suit. They swarmed him and he panicked at the sight of what he thought were aliens. When he fell, they ripped holes in his suit looking for the water."

"When I captured one of the koalas, Dr. Harrington realized they could survive outside the dome."

"Yes," Rawling said. "Remember, I said I would get him to help us. Only instead of helping, he took over the operation. I didn't have much choice. Not when he patched me by radio-phone to a high government source on Earth who forced me to cooperate in trying to hide the existence of these things. When Neilson woke up from his coma, he was also threatened and forced to lie. And from that point on, I was effectively out of it. Nothing to say. Nothing to do."

"That's why you wrote the letter of resignation."

"Yes. And no."

I squinted, puzzled.

"Tyce, I couldn't believe these experiments were simply to create a future food source. Think about it. Once the scientists learned to genetically alter animals to live on the surface of Mars, do you think they'd leave it at that? Or would they try to alter humans next? That's where all this genetic stuff gets scary. Knowledge itself is not good or evil. It's what people choose to do with it. Between Steven and Harrington and the high government source on Earth, you've already seen what can happen. I have no doubt that future genetic technology would be used on humans. But not on adult humans who have a choice."

I let out a deep breath. "On human embryos, right? Because that's where the DNA changes have to be made."

"Exactly. My decision yesterday was to take all of this public. But only if you decided I should. That's why I was looking for you when the screaming started."

"Me? Why should it be up to me?" I asked, stunned by the responsibility he was giving me. After all, I was just a kid.

Rawling got up again. Walked around the room. Sat down.

"Tyce, I know you hate being in a wheelchair. I know how much it means to you to have the freedom of that robot body. You're the first human in history to be given that kind of opportunity."

Rawling's lips tightened in anger. "As director, I had the power to stop the experimentation. I had the power to bring it to light. And I definitely should have done what was right instead of trying to cover it up and hide it from you."

"What does this have to do with the fact that it was going to be my decision?"

"I was being blackmailed. I was told that if I didn't find a way to keep these experiments secret, you'd be sent back to Earth when the shuttle left in a few months. Away from your family. Away from all you are about to learn on Mars. Away from the freedom of that robot body."

"You . . . were . . . covering . . . this . . . up . . . to . . . protect . . . me." The words came slowly out of my mouth.

"I thought I was. Until I realized something. You of all people know what it's like to be experimented on without permission. And here I was, making another decision about you and your future without your knowledge. That was as wrong as covering up what I knew about the experiment."

He looked me square in the eyes. "I hope you can forgive me."

"Sure," I said. "We're friends."

Even as I spoke, I was haunted by guilt. I don't know what I would have decided. Keep my freedom and allow the illegal experiments to continue? Or give up that precious freedom and do what was right—make the experiments public knowledge? I was just glad the decision had been taken from me by Ashley's great screaming job in front of the secret lab.

CHAPTER 27

Half an hour later, I was back in our mini-dome. Mom had already left for her lab. That left me, my father, and the two little Martian koalas. They were asleep in a box in the corner. As usual. Koalas on Earth sleep twenty-two hours a day, and one of the reasons that species had been picked for experiments on Mars was the low amount of energy they burned.

I had things to do, too, like trying to find Ashley to tell her what I'd found out from Rawling.

But I needed to speak to my father first.

On my way past the sleeping koalas, I stopped and smiled. Their eyes were squinted shut, and they made tiny snoring noises.

I had that smile on my face when I stopped in front of my father. He was drinking coffee and reviewing some technical notes when I cleared my throat.

"Dad?" That word came out of my mouth as a surprise. I was so used to thinking of him as "my father," like some uncaring person who bossed me around whenever he showed up.

But I hadn't been able to stop thinking about what he'd said to Rawling in the lab.

Let me tell you this. Mess with Tyce, and you mess with me. Got it? As Tyce's dad, I won't fight his battles for him, but I'll fight his battles with *him.*

"Dad?" I said again. It felt less strange.

He still held his coffee. But his eyes were on my face, not on the technical notes.

"Yesterday," I began, "I was really hurt about something. Rawling suddenly decided not to talk to me, and I couldn't figure out why. It was like we suddenly weren't friends anymore. Only I had no choice about it."

"I'm sorry to hear that," my father said.

"It's all right now," I explained. "We had a chance to talk about it."

"Good."

"Yes. And no."

Dad gave me a strange look. Probably the same strange look I'd given Rawling when he'd used those same words a half hour earlier.

"Good because I found out he had a reason for what he did. Bad because it hit me that I'd been doing the same thing to someone else. You."

Dad set his coffee down.

"You see," I said, "it's not fair for me to do my best to ignore you because I'm mad about stuff. If you have no idea why I'm mad, you probably feel the way I did when Rawling treated me as if I didn't exist."

Dad smiled, but he looked sad. "Now that you mention it . . ."

"Anyway," I said, "I'm sorry."

"Me too," he said. "Do you want to talk about what's bothering you?"

"How much time you got?"

"As much as you need," he said. "Let's talk."

EPILOGUE

Dad and I did talk. Lots.

Over the next month, we became friends again.

Of course, other things happened too.

Rawling tried to resign, but his resignation wasn't accepted. The surviving koalas were allowed to live. Harrington and the ex-director were both scheduled to be sent back to Earth when the next shuttle headed back.

And, oh yeah. Ashley and I spent a lot of time hanging out together.

In fact, things were just settling back to normal—as normal as anything might be for humans living under the dome on Mars—when an earthquake hit.

Well, not an earthquake.

This was Mars. I guess you'd have to call it a "Marsquake."

Whatever it was, it was scary. Although it happened at least two hundred miles away, it still rocked the dome.

What was even scarier was the fact that it might not have been an accident.

But all this, of course, is going to fill another diary. . . .

THE HOW
AND WHY OF LIFE

Have you ever wondered, like Tyce Sanders, how you came to be you and why you exist?

As a human being, you're made up of one trillion cells.

How much is one trillion? To hold one trillion oranges, you'd need a box that's 250 miles long, 250 miles wide, and 250 miles high!

Even more amazingly, all these cells work together. Some cells grow hair; some grow teeth. Some cells don't begin to work until you become a teenager. Other cells wait until you're middle-aged. You have blood cells, heart muscle cells, liver cells, eye cells, brain neuron cells, and more.

Most amazing, all one trillion cells are the result of the one cell created when you were conceived. As Tyce's mom explained to him, the DNA in this first cell contains every bit of information needed for your body to grow.

What exactly is DNA? Deoxyribonucleic acid. It's life's building block.

DNA is shaped like a spiral staircase. In a human, the DNA ladder in one cell contains three billion "rungs." (If DNA was the size of a real ladder, those three billion rungs

119

would circle the entire Earth—twice. Wow. Think about that!)

Because of its shape, DNA is able to replicate itself perfectly. When a cell needs to make a copy of itself, the DNA "ladder" unzips down the middle to form two halves. The result is two exact copies of the original. That's how one cell at conception can pass on the exact copy of its DNA to all trillion cells of a human.

Each different cell is able to specialize because it activates a different section of the DNA "ladder." These sections are called genes. Some genes trigger a cell to become hair cells. Other genes trigger a cell to become blood cells. And so on.

In one way, this method is extremely simple. After scientists discovered the "double helix" shape of DNA and everything else about it, they were able to run many experiments, including the ones mentioned by Tyce's mother.

In another way, however, DNA is overwhelmingly incredible. The information stored in the DNA of just one cell would fill the hard drives of a million personal computers. The microscopic chemical reactions resulting from the DNA coding happen millions of times a day in your body.

DNA is so incredible that many scientists find it very difficult to believe that life was the result of accidental evolution. Like Tyce's mom, these scientists cannot help but look to God as our Creator.

After all, life itself is a humbling mystery.

Think of it this way. We survive because of sunlight and water and dirt. Our bodies are nourished by carbohydrates from bread, which comes from wheat, which draws from moisture and sunlight and soil. Our bodies are strengthened by protein from the meat of animals, which feed upon plants. All of this is made possible by the water that falls from the skies and collects in rivers and lakes.

Sunlight, water, and dirt.

We forget how incredible it is because we see it and live it every day and give it little thought. We plunk down a few dollars for our hamburgers at a drive-through; we pick up milk from the grocery store; the sun throws off heat from 93 million miles away; the Earth remains in its fixed distance from the sun—not too close, not too far, held by gravity that we can predict but not explain.

If you think of life this way, it's not hard to believe that such a world with such mystery exists because of the unseen hand of a Creator.

All of this leads to a much bigger question: why?

Although learning "how" we're on this earth is fascinating, learning "why" we're really here is the most wonderful purpose given to us as humans. As Tyce discovered, that journey involves a search through faith—and learning what it means to be in a world created by a powerful yet personal God who loves you more than life itself.

ABOUT THE AUTHOR

Sigmund Brouwer and his wife, recording artist Cindy Morgan, split living between Red Deer, Alberta, Canada, and Nashville, Tennessee. He has written several series of juvenile fiction and eight novels. Sigmund loves sports and plays golf and hockey. He also enjoys visiting schools to talk about books. He welcomes visitors to his Web site at www.coolreading.com, where he and a bunch of other authors like to hang out in cyberspace.

MARS
DIARIES
are you ready?

Set in an experimental community on Mars in the years 2039–2043, the Mars Diaries feature teen virtual-reality specialist Tyce Sanders. Life on the red planet is not always easy, but it is definitely exciting. As Tyce explores his strange surroundings, he also finds that the mysteries of the planet point to his greatest discovery—a new relationship with God.

MISSION 1: OXYGEN LEVEL ZERO
Time was running out...

MISSION 2: ALIEN PURSUIT
"Help me!" And the radio went dead....

MISSION 3: TIME BOMB
A quake rocks the red planet, uncovering a long kept secret....

MISSION 4: HAMMERHEAD
I was dead center in the laser target controls....

MISSION 5: SOLE SURVIVOR
Scientists buried alive at cave-in site!

MISSION 6: MOON RACER
Everyone has a motive...and secrets. The truth must be found before it's too late.

MISSION 7: COUNTDOWN
20 soldiers, 20 neuron rifles. There was nowhere to run.
Nowhere to hide...

MISSION 8: ROBOT WAR
Ashley and I are their only hope, and they think we're traitors.

MISSION 9: MANCHURIAN SECTOR
I was in trouble...and I couldn't trust anyone.

MISSION 10: LAST STAND
Invasion was imminent ... and we'd lost all contact with Earth.